Here Ghost Nothing

LIA PRESTON

LUNARIA PRESS, INC.

Second Edition

Print ISBN: 978-1-7388946-2-8

Cover: Lunaria Cover Design
Editing: Eyes on Your Story

Published in Canada by Lunaria Press, Inc.

Part One

Chapter 1

Piper

"What do you think these are?" I poked at the punch bowl with the spoon and looked over at Bianca. The translucent orbs bobbed, grotesque among the deep red juice.

"Skinned grapes, I think. Avoid them."

"Oh, believe me, I plan on it. On second thought, maybe we should just go grab some wine from the bar?"

Besides, I needed something to soothe my nerves.

She pushed her blonde curls over her shoulder. "Sounds like a plan to me. Sometimes free just isn't worth it."

"Agreed."

I scanned the room and took a deep breath, noticing the long line-up for the bar.

Okay, forget that idea.

I was too thirsty to wait that long. The woman in line behind us put her hands on her hips and tapped her foot.

"Sorry, I'll be quick." I turned, scooped two spoonfuls of punch into a cup for me and two into one for Bianca, and darted out of the way. "It's all yours," I said to the woman.

She ignored me and poured herself some punch.

Aren't small-town people supposed to be friendlier?

I was used to dealing with my fair share of rudeness in Los Angeles, but I'd hoped that this trip would be a break from the norm. I looked up at the clock on the wall of the hall. It was a quarter past nine and there was still no sign of him. I wondered what the hold-up was. I readjusted my masquerade mask, making sure it was secure.

Zane wouldn't recognize me with or without it, but his sister, Zara, might.

I couldn't afford to be noticed tonight of all nights. I straightened the black and yellow striped bodice of the bee costume I'd borrowed from Bianca. Well, an anthropomorphized bee, since the last time I checked, bees didn't wear fishnets or yellow tutus.

I scanned the room again for Zane. Where was he?

My heart hammered when I thought about him—it always did.

I just had to see him one more time.

One more time would have to serve me until things could change—if it wasn't too late by then.

But it had to be this way *for his sake*.

Bianca and I both ordered a glass of rosé from the bar. Bianca hooked her arm in mine.

I smiled over at her. "Thanks for coming with me. I appreciate it."

"Anytime. But you know that."

I nodded and took a sip from my wine glass.

Bianca had been my closest friend for many years. My father directed most of the cooking shows her father starred in when we were younger and we'd met on set when she was nine and I was eight.

We found a booth to sit at and I sighed, taking another sip of my wine.

Bianca tapped me on my shoulder and leaned in. "There he is."

I turned to match her gaze and sucked in a breath, my heart thumping in my chest. It was him all right, but he looked different.

He was wearing jeans and a plaid shirt. He'd always been a casual dresser, even in L.A., but he looked right at home in country boy clothing. Then again, Weston was his childhood home. But those jeans, boy, was he filling them out just right. My eyes ran the length of his body.

Memories of what his body could do heated my core to where, if I didn't look away, I thought I might combust where I stood. But I couldn't force myself to. Old habits were hard to break, and Zane Merrick was the hardest of all.

He ran his hand through his almost black hair. It had grayed more since I'd last seen him. Was that genetic or the stress of the accident? As he approached the bar, he ordered, then turned around, scanning the room with his dark eyes.

I glanced down at my glass and traced the rim with my fingertip. What I wouldn't give to look right into his eyes again.

But you can't.

To be subject to his gaze, and the way he once looked at me like I was his entire world.

That was *before* our hopes and dreams went up in smoke.

Halloween night was supposed to be spooky fun, but all that haunted me was the way things could have been. The way our lives should have been.

Bianca squeezed my shoulder. "Are you sure you're going to be okay?"

I gave Zane another quick glance as he took a bottle of beer from the bartender and swigged from it.

Was I going to be okay?

No, never. Not as long as I had to live without him. But I had no choice.

"It's strange seeing him again."

"I bet it is. Why you wanted to do this in the first place, I'm not sure. It seems like a pretty rotten way to spend your birthday. Aren't you—" She paused and frowned. "—torturing yourself?"

And maybe I was. But love costs you sometimes, and I'd paid the ultimate price. I was bankrupt. It might have been my twenty-third birthday, but celebrating was the farthest thing from my mind.

"It's hard. But I needed to see him."

"And you have now. So?"

I sucked in a breath. We'd come a long way for a glance, but Bee was right. "Okay, let's go."

"Are you sure? I don't want to be pushy, but I think it might be for the best."

I tipped back the rest of my wine. "Yes, I agree. Finish your drink. I have to go to the washroom, and then we'll leave."

She lifted her glass. "On it."

I slipped out of the booth and headed for the washroom. I tried the door but it was locked so I stepped back and leaned against the wall to wait for my turn.

What was I thinking coming here?

Zane had a new life—or his old life back—considering

he grew up in Weston. It was really confusing. The life we had shared in Los Angeles was starting to feel like more of a figment of my imagination, especially seeing that the only person who was incapable of moving on from it was me.

A man came stumbling around the corner. His shoulder slammed into the wall and he eyed me and let out a low whistle before slithering along the wall to stand next to me.

"Damn, well, isn't it my lucky night?" he sneered.

I turned away from him and didn't respond.

"Cat got your tongue?" I felt his face in my hair, followed by a loud sniff. "Fuck, you smell so good."

I pushed away from the wall. "I was just leaving." My bladder would have to wait until Bee and I got back to the hotel. This mission was a bust anyhow.

He stepped in front of me and pushed me back toward the wall. "The night's young. Stay." He ran his hand up my outer thigh. "I'll make it worth your while."

His beady eyes were cold and unfocused.

My heart hammered in my chest. I pushed him back far enough to escape.

He pulled me back, caging me against the wall once again.

"Leave me alone," I said, my voice quivering.

"Give me a little kis—"

Just then, his body reared back, slamming into the bathroom door. A tall blur of plaid stepped between him and me. "Are you not fucking hearing her? She said to leave her alone."

"Stay out of this," the drunk snarled as he regained his footing.

A lump formed in my throat when I realized who'd come to my rescue.

Zane.

The one man I couldn't afford to cross paths with was standing right in mine—protecting me.

As he once promised, he always would.

And if I hadn't already loved him, I would have fallen for him in that instant.

Chapter 2

Zane

"You better get the fuck outta here."

"Make me, dickhead."

I stepped toward him and cocked my fist. He startled and slid down the wall, half crawling down the hall until he regained his footing and disappeared around the corner.

That was easy.

I turned to face the woman he'd harassed. "You all right, Miss?"

Her breath hitched at my addressing her before she nodded. She was still in shock from what she'd just endured. I reached for her and she flinched.

It was clear she didn't want to be touched. Of course, she didn't, not after what she'd just been through.

"I'm sorry. I didn't mean to give you a fright. Hey, the sheriff is in the other room. I'll have him arrested."

"No, no, I'll be okay. Umm, thank you, uh…" she trailed off.

"Zane. Did you know him?"

Please tell me a woman as beautiful as her wasn't involved with a creep like him? I'd seen it many times in my years, working as a firefighter. Houses went up in literal flames from psychotic fuckers like that.

She glanced around. "I—I need to go." Her full lips pouted at me. "Thanks again."

I didn't want to leave her side. As she was still shaken up, but what other choice did I have? "Well, if you need anything, come and find me, all right?"

Her eyes locked with mine and she put her hand on her hip. "That's very chivalrous of you but I'll be all right"

"It's not too late, you know. I'll chase him down myself."

She sighed, relaxing back against the wall. "Tempting. But I'm leaving town tomorrow. It would be a hassle tying me to this town that I don't need."

It disappointed me to hear that she was just passing through. I'd hoped this wouldn't be our first and last chance encounter, but the odds seemed stacked against me. "What brings you to a dusty desert town like Weston?"

I knew what had brought me to the middle of nowhere in Arizona. My sister. Well, not only my sister, but my recovery and my sister's insistence on helping me through it. I'd spent countless hours at doctor's appointments and in rehabilitation after the accident.

There was a point when I couldn't wait to get back to the coast, but why? I'd been in Weston for a year and while I hadn't put down roots I wondered what was drawing me back to Los Angeles.

She ran a blonde lock of hair through her fingers. It

looked as smooth as a satin ribbon. "I'm just here to visit an old friend."

"Oh? Not that guy, I hope." I pointed over my shoulder in the general direction of his retreat.

She laughed, glancing over at the washroom as the woman inside vacated it. "Not a chance. I have to use the washroom, Zane, it was nice to meet—"

"Have a drink with me?" I interjected, not wanting her to finish that sentence. Because her ending the sentence meant it was the end of us. If there was an 'us'.

There was something about this woman that made me want to know her better. And it wasn't just her perfect curves or her stunning beauty, at least that is what I was telling myself. There was something about her I couldn't quite put my finger on.

Her eyes darted around. I followed her gaze, wondering what she was looking for. That guy wasn't likely to return soon if that's what she was worried about. "Look, I need to get out of here, but give me an hour, and if you want to have that drink, come to the Weston Inn room..." She bit her lip. "Room 204, okay?"

I raised my eyebrows at her. It was forward of her, but also sexy. How could I say no? "You've got it, Miss?"

"P—Honey."

I scanned her, and the sexy little bumble bee costume she wore. "I see how it is, Miss Honey."

She gave me a wide smile before pushing away from the wall and disappearing into the washroom. How had we gone from her leaving to me getting an invitation back to her hotel room? Maybe this was how she operated?

She didn't seem like the sort. But it was a bit of a dangerous move. Not with me, but she didn't know me. It didn't matter though, it was a chance to get to know more about her and there was no way I was going to let that pass me by.

It'd been years since I'd been with a woman. My sister told me that even before my accident I hadn't been in a serious relationship in a while. There must have been someone, though, because when I'd returned home, I'd found traces of a woman. But that was it.

Whoever she was didn't seem to want to stick around for a guy that doctors were saying might never walk again thanks to the spinal damage I'd encountered.

So, maybe I was better off not remembering who'd left those behind. My sister, Zara, had tried to say it was her hairbrush when she snatched it away from me. But the few blonde hairs twisted through the bristles showed otherwise. I made my way down the hall and back to my table where my sister Zara and her husband Mark sat. She'd been trying to protect me. I hadn't pushed the issue because I had bigger things to concern myself with.

But none of that mattered anymore.

Los Angeles felt like it was a lifetime ago—what I could remember of it, anyhow.

I returned to our table, where Zara took a sip of her drink. "Where did you disappear to?"

I smiled. "Just the washroom."

Where I'd met the most beautiful woman in the world and I was about to go meet up with her in a hotel room.

After a year of rotten luck, it seemed like things were about to turn around.

Chapter 3

Piper

"Are you insane? We need to leave right now." Bee paced the floor of my room.

"Maybe. But you really need to go to your own room. He'll be here any minute."

If he showed.

Zane was never the sort to agree to a random hookup and even though there was nothing 'random' about me he didn't know that. Which meant the chances of him showing were slim-to-none.

"This wasn't part of the plan, Piper. You said you wanted to see him one last time. You saw him. Leave it at that."

She was right, that *was* the plan. "Plans change."

She sat on the end of the bed. "You're playing a dangerous game. Is it worth risking it all by inviting Zane back here?"

I sat down next to her and cradled my head in my hands. "It was the way he was looking at me. I just need this, okay? One night and I'll let him go."

What I really wanted to tell her was the lack of recognition in his eyes killed me inside. Why couldn't I have lost my memory too? Why did I have to be the one burdened with every moment we'd spent together only for our world to be splintered apart? I just wanted him to know me again. Even if it was only in the form of one night.

Bee sighed and reached out to rub my back. "I knew this was going to be too tough. But if it's what you need, I'll support you."

Bianca was right. It was a risk I shouldn't have been taking but things had gone how they had. And I had an opportunity for us to share one memory. I craved that more than I could even put into words. One forbidden memory and I'd behave. I had no other choice but to leave it at that. "I appreciate that. Now you really must go. I told him one hour and it was Zane. If he isn't five minutes early I'd be surprised."

***

I was *SURPRISED.*

I waited an extra twenty-five minutes after Bianca had left before I heard a rap at the door.

When I saw his face through the door's peephole I was almost certain it wouldn't be Zane standing on the other side. He'd never been one to be late before. Then again, old Zane never would have shown up to something like this. I had to remind myself that the Zane I once knew was likely a changed man and that I couldn't rely on everything being the same as it once was.

Not that it mattered.

We had tonight, and only tonight.

I unlocked the door and opened it. "Hey, come in. I was starting to think you weren't coming."

He glanced around the parking lot and then my suite before stepping in.

"Sorry I'm late. My sister wouldn't let me leave until they announced the winner of the costume contest. She takes this stuff pretty seriously."

I smiled. He always was a sucker for his twin sister, Zara. They'd lost their parents when they were young in a house fire and had been raised right here by their grandparents in Weston. Zara never left and married her high-school sweetheart. But Zane had moved to Los Angeles with a few friends after high school to become a firefighter. "That's okay. I'm glad you came."

He furrowed his brow. "About that. What are we doing here, exactly?"

A snap of cold raced through me. I'd hoped he wouldn't ask me too many questions. What I'd done was abrupt, foolish even. Even I could see how little sense it made at the moment. We'd only exchanged a few words. Far too few to warrant me inviting him back to my room, but that's what I'd done and he actually showed. "I—I got the feeling you wanted to hang out some more. And after what happened I wasn't feeling like staying there." I wrung my fingers in my other hand. "Sorry, if I read the situation wrong you can go. I didn't mean to—"

"You're cute when you're flustered," he chuckled and pulled the door from my hand, which I hadn't realized I'd still been holding open, and stepped further into the room to let it fall closed behind him.

The room felt smaller with him in it. Like there was nowhere else to be except near him. I was grateful for it but terrified at the same time.

What if I couldn't let him go again?

He slipped a backpack off his shoulder and bent over to unzip it. He pulled a bottle of sparkling rosé from his bag. The same kind I was drinking with Bianca earlier. One of my favorites. How did he know?

Did he—

My heart hammered in my chest at the possibility.

Did he remember me? Is that why he'd come?

He ran a hand through his hair. "I asked the bartender what you were drinking and brought you a bottle. We can share it if the mood strikes, or if that's not where the night takes us, you can share it with your *friend* later. It's up to you." I could tell by the way he said friend he was fishing for details, details I couldn't give, as he extended the bottle to me. It was a sweet gesture, but I couldn't help but be disappointed that he'd had to ask the bartender. Even though I knew I shouldn't have hoped for anything more than that. As I took the bottle from him, his eyes were still searching mine for answers.

Snap out of it, Piper.

I was ruining this last night with my brooding. "Thank you," I said and turned to put it in the mini-fridge. "I'll chill it for a bit and then maybe we can have a glass or two together."

"Sounds like a plan." He toured around the room and looped back to me. "Honey, I'm not sure what I'm doing here. But I know I want to be here—that I should be here. Does that make sense to you?"

My heart was in my throat. I wanted to croak out something, it couldn't be the truth but anything of value would have done. He stepped toward me and my breathing hitched.

His eyes narrowed. "I think you're feeling it too. And I

know I should suggest we watch a movie or something but there's only one thing I want to do right now."

I swallowed hard. He was so close. "And what's that?"

"This." He wrapped his arm around my waist and pulled me flush to him. His lips descended on mine. I should have pushed back but I couldn't do it. Instead, I pressed my body against his, letting my hand tangle in his salt-and-pepper hair. He was thirty-six, much older than me at twenty-two, but he'd always been the most handsome man I'd ever known. He deepened the kiss and let out a low groan into my mouth. My body shuddered thinking back to all the other times I'd heard him make a noise like that. I'd felt so incomplete without him for the past year. I'd been living with a void that only Zane could fill for me and being back in his arms only proved that further.

He broke the kiss and pressed his forehead to mine. "Sorry, I've wanted to do that since the moment I set eyes on you. It just didn't seem like the right time."

I laughed. If he only knew how long I'd been waiting to feel his lips against mine again. "No need to be sorry, I liked it."

He smiled and gave me a few more quick kisses before groaning again. "What do you want to do now?"

I bit my lip. "More of the same?"

He grabbed my ass, and hoisted me up. As I wrapped my legs around his hips, he carried me to the bed. He was the only man I'd ever met that had the strength to lift me like that. "I can't argue with that," he said before his lips met mine again.

He was the love of my life, even if he didn't know it anymore, and all I wanted to do was drown in his affections—one last time.

Chapter 4

Zane

She arched her back and locked her legs around my hips as she ground against my hard cock. There was something so sexy about how fearless she was in my arms. Like she felt at home in them. How I got so lucky, I wasn't sure. She was stunning. I was curious why we ended up here, but a part of me wanted to not care. All I wanted was my mouth on her body and to be buried deep inside her.

What was it about this woman?

She tore desires from me I hadn't felt about anyone for as long as I could remember. The urge to make her mine commanded me. I reared back. This wasn't me. I owed her the courtesy of getting to know her first, didn't I?

"Don't stop," she said, her voice a sultry whisper.

I couldn't deny her lips their wish, so I kissed her again.

"I don't want to take advantage of you," I said between kisses.

"You aren't. I promise. Just please don't stop. I need you."

I scanned her face, searching for reasons to say no. A hint of doubt. A waver of decision. There was nothing except her beauty and desire that met me. I slipped my hand between us beneath the bright yellow skirt of her costume and slipped my fingers beneath the side hem of her panties.

She was so fucking wet that it was unreal. "Is this what you need?" I said, massaging her clit with my fingertips.

'Yes, please, yes," she moaned as her body shivered beneath mine.

Her guard was up except for the way her body called out to mine. What would it do when met with my powerful thrusts? Would they be enough to break her of her alias? Could I make her stay a while longer instead of leaving town in the morning?

There was only one way to find out.

I rolled off her in search of my bag and fished out a condom. I would have loved to bury myself into her bare. To claim her as my own. But I couldn't.

Not without knowing her name first.

The consequences of that were too steep. I was already pushing my boundaries, succumbing to this woman in the way I was. I didn't want to lose any more control than I already had.

She shimmied out of her panties as I tore the package and palmed my erection before rolling the condom on.

I positioned myself back between her legs, like a man kneeling in front of an altar prepared for worship. "And you're sure this is what you want?"

She smiled up at me. "Positive."

I thrust myself inside her, ripping a moan from her lips that was as satisfying to my ears as her wet, warm pussy was around my cock.

I steeled myself for it. The unrelenting feel of her walls around my shaft. The tightness had my eyes rolling back in my head. I wanted to fuck her like an animal. To make her feel every inch of me. "Damn," I said, releasing a breath of air I'd been holding. And then I began fucking her. Deep, hard thrusts. I watched her face.

Her eyes slammed closed and her mouth formed a perfect 'o'.

"You're so fucking tight," I groaned as I gripped her hips.

Propelling her into me, impaling her on my cock with every punishing drive. I thrust into her again, harder than the last. Her body bowed, her eyes fluttered, and her mouth fell open as she gasped. "Ahh," she moaned.

The tiny sound of pleasure sent vibrations running through me. I gripped her ass so hard it might leave a mark.

The sensitive skin of her pussy gripped me like a prize. My orgasm careened toward the edge faster than I'd ever remembered experiencing before. She was so fucking tight.

"Oh, god," she moaned. "You're so deep." Her breaths quickened, infused with lust.

She was right. I was deep.

Deep inside my personal hell.

I wanted this to last. Wanted to savor it and her. More than anything I wanted her to remember this night. Because when it ended and she left, who knew if it would be the last of her I'd see? Would it ever happen again?

I pumped into her harder. She met each of my thrusts with a moan or a gasp. "Ahh," she cried out.

Her back arched and a light sheen of sweat covered her body. I gripped her hair, tugging her head.

"Yes," she cried out. "More." I held her body against mine. My thrusts came fast and hard.

I felt myself getting close.

Her body was on fire, drenching me in her desire. I pumped into her one more time and then I couldn't control it anymore. With one final thrust into her, my release poured into the condom. My cock pulsed with hot hunger with an intensity that I hadn't felt in years.

It was mind-numbing. I grunted, savoring every moment of my pleasure. As I slid out of her the cool air on my cock made me crave her depths again.

But I'd settled for holding her in my arms. She nuzzled her face into my shoulder until her eyes fluttered closed and her breathing deepened.

And I knew at that moment I'd do anything in my power to keep her close if only she'd allow it.

Sure, we'd only met, but there was a nagging in the back of my mind that insisted she was meant to be mine that arrived the moment I'd laid eyes on Honey.

And if she didn't feel the same yet, come morning, I'd make damn sure she couldn't feel any other way about it.

Chapter 5

Piper

I awoke to the sound of my silenced phone buzzing against the table next to me. My heart sank when I saw the word 'Dad' on the screen. A middle-of-the-night call could mean only one thing.

My secret rendezvous wasn't so secret anymore.

I pressed end call, dressed, and packed my bag. Thankful that Zane was as sound of a sleeper as he'd always been.

My heart ached as I looked at his face, illuminated only by a small strip of moonlight that shone through the crack in the curtains.

We'd both fallen asleep after sex. The wine never made it out of the fridge. It had been the most restful sleep I'd had in years. What I wouldn't give to revisit his arms night after night like we used to.

Being near him had stitched my heart in ways I hadn't imagined one night could. A lump formed in my throat because I had no other choice but to tear them all out and reopen the wound, knowing it would be worse this time.

I zipped my bag shut and found the complimentary notepad and pen provided by the hotel and wrote.

Zane,

I wish I could tell you why I need to leave. You more than deserve an explanation, but I can't give it to you yet. When the time is right, I'll return to the Halloween Gala and I hope to see you there.

Thank you for making this the best birthday I could have ever hoped for. There's so much more I wish I could say, and I hope I'll get the chance to someday soon.

Yours truly,
Honey

It was a terrible letter to write and not even close to being enough. But it was all I could say. Even though I knew it was for the best, my insides churned as I tip-toed to the bedside table to leave the note.

His hand shot out, grasping my wrist, and startled me. "What are you doing?" he mumbled, his eyes still closed. I could hear my phone buzzing from within my purse. I had to make this quick.

"Take this," I said, removing his hand from my arm

and pressing the note into his palm before curling his fingers. "Everything you need to know is there." I gave his cheek a light kiss. My throat burned as tears welled in my eyes. "Go back to sleep now," I ordered, although I wasn't sure he was even awake, to begin with.

He turned over in the bed and the note crumpled in his palm. I grabbed my overnight bag and slipped out of the room into the crisp fall night.

I hurried to Bee's room and swiped the spare room card she'd given me. The sound of the door clicking closed startled her awake.

"Piper, wha—" She rubbed at her eyes. "What's wrong?"

I flopped down on the bed next to her and fished my phone from my purse.

"My father's calling me. Which can only mean one thing."

"Oh no," she said with a sigh.

I returned his call, pressing the phone to my ear. "Hi Dad, you called?"

"It took you long enough to answer, Piper."

"Sorry, I was asleep."

"Is that what we're calling it these days? It's been brought to my attention that you've made a trip to Arizona."

"Yes, Father." There was no point in telling him a lie at this point. I knew him well enough to know that he'd never confront me without gathering all the facts first.

"I thought we'd agreed that you'd stay away from him."

"We did. I'm sorry. I just wanted to see him once more. And I know I shouldn't have, but—"

"No, you shouldn't have. You're putting our agreement in jeopardy, but you know that."

"I do."

He sighed. "That man's not right for you, my dear. You know this. But I can't say I didn't expect that this would happen. I'll let it slide this once. But know that if you can't keep to the agreement, there will be consequences for *everyone* involved—especially him."

When my father had learned of Zane and my involvement, he'd cautioned me against the intentions of an older man with a woman of my age. That he was only after me for my money. I tried to explain to him that Zane wasn't like that. That we were in love and I intended to be with him. And I had until the accident. Then everything changed in an instant.

"You have my word. I won't do it again."

"Good, I trust you'll be home in the morning, then?"

"I will."

"Excellent. Come over for dinner. I'd like to celebrate my only daughter's birthday with her this year."

"Of course."

We said goodnight, and I rolled over to face Bianca. "Well, at least I didn't screw everything up."

She scrunched her nose. "How are you feeling? Are you okay?"

I closed my eyes. I couldn't even answer her. Maybe in time, the ache would lessen. I knew I was doing the best I could. But it didn't make it hurt any less. Knowing that the man I loved was just on the other side of the wall and that I'd seen him for what might be the last time tore me up inside. I felt like I was going to be ill. "We need to go."

"Now?"

"Yes, now. I'm sorry. This was all a huge mistake."

She slipped out of bed. "Okay, I'll pack my things and charter a jet. You call for a ride to the airport."

I didn't know what I would do without Bianca. She was

a planner by nature and she knew how to take charge even
when things were falling apart.

And at that moment, I was in pieces.

Part Two

THREE YEARS LATER

Chapter One

ZANE

Two arms slipped around my bare shoulders. I could tell she was on her tip-toes by how her body leaned into mine for support. I reached behind and ran my hand over her thigh. Her smooth skin warmed my palm. My interest grew as I stirred the Alfredo sauce with my free hand one last time before sliding it off the element.

It was her favorite meal and tonight of all nights had to be perfect.

I knew what I'd see before I even turned around. We spent a lot of nights together like this and she always wore the same relaxed expression. Her long blonde hair fell around her shoulders in waves. It was thick, just like the rest of her petite yet curvy body, and I loved running my fingers through her silken strands.

Oh, who was I kidding?

I loved every inch of her. She was a masterpiece of a woman.

But an impatient one.

"You couldn't wait to seduce me until I finished making dinner?"

She pouted, her eyes dancing over my exposed chest as she walked two fingers down it toward the waistband of my lounge pants. "Maybe I'm not feeling hungry yet."

I reached around her and gripped each meaty thigh where it met the curve of her ass, cradling it in the palm of my hands.

The naughty girl was naked underneath the short dress she wore. My fingers dipped into her wetness as I lifted her up to seat her on the marble countertop.

"Oh." She shuffled. "That's cold."

"Good, you could use a little cooling off." Thankfully, I had a smidge more self-control than she did, but that didn't stop me from getting hard at the feel of her. I rubbed my wet fingertips together, looked up, and reached out for her. "You left something behind." I put my fingers to her lips, she parted them, and I popped them into her mouth before she sucked them clean.

A fire raged within me, fueled by my lust for her. But it was the way she mirrored the same desire back to me that told me one thing for certain.

She was mine.

All fucking mine.

I cleared my throat, fighting off the temptation to ruin my surprise.

I wondered what it was…

What had I planned to surprise her with?

How odd, I was drawing a complete blank.

"It's ready. Are you sure I can't interest you in it while it's fresh? I added basil, just like you like. Even though it's—"

"I know, I know, it's not Alfredo sauce then. But who cares? That's the way I like it. And, fine, I'll eat a bite or two." I was all for giving things to her just how she liked them, so I sank my teeth into the soft hollow of her neck.

She gasped. "Again."

"No. A taste for a taste. It's only fair."

When I turned to slide the drawer open to grab a spoon, I furrowed my brow.

That's strange.

It was empty except for a little black box. I reached into the drawer and pulled it out. There was something I was supposed to do with it.

I knew that much for sure.

Turning the little box over in my hand I remembered I'd tucked it away in the drawer for this very moment. It was too flat to be a ring box, so an engagement ring was out of the question.

Or was it?

Or were we already engaged?

It felt like we should have been.

She was leaning back on her hands when I glanced back at her. Her ring finger was out of sight.

I turned to face her. Whatever was in the box must've been hers. I held it out to her and a searing pain shot through my head. It was so sharp and direct it felt like an arrow had pierced my left temple and exited through the right.

I grabbed my head, my vision blurring from the impact. The box slipped from my grip but the sound of it hitting the floor didn't follow.

"Zane, are you sure?" I struggled to see the smile on her lips as she looked up from the box in her hands. Her face was obscured by a thick fog surrounding us.

No, it wasn't fog. The smell of burning plastic and wood filled the air. I knew that smell all too well from my years working for the fire department. It was smoke, but not just any smoke. Though I couldn't see it, I knew the house was on fire.

"We have to get out of here." I coughed out. The cloud was so dense between us I couldn't see her anymore, but I heard her laugh.

"Babe, you're such a tease. You said you weren't ready last week."

How could she remain calm at a time like this? When I reached through the smoke, I grabbed her by the waist and threw her over my shoulder. I looked down at my chest. The bare skin she'd been caressing only minutes before was now covered by full turnout gear. I felt relieved to see I was ready for action.

I had to be quick, but I could get her out of there safely. "Everything's going to be okay." She felt limp and light on my shoulder as I gripped her harder. I looked over to find my jacket draped where she'd once been.

My mouth fell open. I wanted to call out to her, but I didn't know her name.

"Sweetie? Are you still in here?"

Silence.

I opened the front door and the sky was orange. I'd only ever seen it look like that when I was in California, and the wildfires were raging. They had sent us out to take shifts trying to control the path of the burn. An act of total futility for even the most experienced of firefighters.

When a fire burns that hot, it's almost impossible to quell until it's ready.

Just like her.

I darted back into the house. She was in there. I knew it. And I had to find her.

Chapter Two

PIPER

"Postpone my ten a.m. appointment. There's an emergency on the studio lot. I need to head down there and see what's going on."

"Of course, Miss Rhodes," Sandra called out to me as I dashed from my office to the stairwell. The elevator would take too long. Antonio, the director, had been vague when I'd tried to question him. He only said he needed me down there as soon as possible.

I hit the bar and the metal door swung open. It was the style of door you might see at a school. Well, not *my* old school. With their crystal stained glass, and antique brass fixtures, a door so pedestrian would have been far beneath them. I often sat in the corner of the student lounge watching the prisms along the wall and counted down the minutes until lunch was over because that meant we were one step closer to going home.

The studio Antonio was in was at the other end of the lot. I hopped in an electric cart and sped down there. I grew up as a studio kid and spent most of the time on the lot surrounded by the cast and crew of whatever project my dad was directing. They educated me on location with child celebrities or children of celebrities. It was how I met my closest friend Bianca. Her dad's a famous chef and my dad directed a few of his TV shows. My mom was an actress.

But when I was in my late teens my grandpa fell ill so my father stepped away from the set and moved into the office. My mother followed suit soon after and they sent me to regular school for a while. I hated it. I'd even taken a role in a teen drama so I could get out of it. Being an actress wasn't for me and so I followed in my parents' footsteps and took on an executive position in the company instead.

Was it for me?

Most days, yes.

The problem was that I didn't know what else I'd be doing if I wasn't working at the studio. It was my life. I'd stepped away from it when I met someone that my father didn't approve of. It was that or face hostility and disappointment daily.

But when that relationship came to a screeching halt I returned with my tail between my legs and resumed my fast track to Chief Financial Officer. And while I enjoyed it, I wanted to have something of my own on the side.

I parked the cart, hopped out, and made my way into the studio. It was pitch black inside.

Had I gone to the wrong one?

No way.

Soft music began to play overhead, and a spotlight

appeared on the set where I saw Myles Reeve seated on a prop sofa from the sitcom he starred in.

I folded my arms across my chest and sighed.

Not again.

"What's going on, Myles? Where's the emergency?"

He stood from the sofa and started toward me. "The emergency is that I'm going to die of a broken heart—" He cupped his hands to his chest for dramatic effect. "—if you don't agree to go out with me."

"You mean your ego can't cope."

He shrugged. "Same thing. You should come out this weekend. We can celebrate your twenty-fifth birthday in style. My treat."

His long, sun-bleached hair was pulled up into a man bun emphasizing his angular cheekbones. He was pretty, but it still didn't change how I felt. "I'm headed out of town."

"Again? You're always too busy, Piper. One of these days I'm just going to stop asking."

"Can that be today? You've disturbed the entire cast and crew with this nonsense. Come out guys, it's time to get back to work." The lights flicked on and the music stopped as people made their way back to the studio floor.

I looked over at Antonio, the director, and shook my head. "And you! I can't believe you allowed this."

He turned his palms skyward. "He was refusing to work unless we went along with it."

I'd believe that. Myles was about as stubborn as they came.

The fact that I said no every time he pulled a stunt like that should have been a solid hint I wasn't interested–but it wasn't. I turned to him and put my hands on my hips. "This can't happen again. It's not appropriate. I'm your boss and—"

"Where are you headed?"

"Arizona." Wait, why did I answer him? My personal life was none of his business.

"Whereabouts?"

"Uh—" I didn't want the word to get around that I'd be in the small town of Weston. "—Tucson."

"Why there?"

"Just a little spa getaway."

He stared at me. It was clear he wanted more of an explanation than I was offering.

I shrugged. "I enjoy the desert."

"We have spas and deserts in California, you know."

"Yes, but anywhere in Cali is close enough for me to be called back to the office."

"You have access to the company's private jet. Anywhere in North America is close enough for you to be called back."

I let out a frustrated huff. "Enough. Get back to work."

He frowned. "You're going to see *him*, aren't you?"

My eyebrow twitched at the casual mention of Zane. People around the studio knew about my past. They knew what had caused my return, but no one ever brought it up, at least not to my face. My throat seized, unable to answer him, but the silence was revealing.

"How do you know he hasn't moved on yet? And even if he hasn't, how do you know there is a connection left between you two?"

"I don't—I mean—I don't need to answer these questions. Get back to work. You're costing the company money standing around."

I spun on my heels and left the studio. Dealing with actors and their egos was par for the course in this industry and if Myles hadn't been the lead actor in our most profitable sitcom, I might've fired him on the spot. He'd move on to other women soon enough. They always seemed to catch interest in the big boss's daughter for a minute or two. And while I'd made the mistake of dating a couple of them before Zane appeared in my life, I knew from those experiences that the attention wasn't genuine and always fleeting. Then again, nothing could compare to what Zane and I had shared. There was no replacing him. He was the only one for me.

Since the accident, I had only seen Zane once. Oh sure, I'd visited the hospital to see him while he was still unconscious, but once he woke up, they denied me access, as requested by his sister, Zara. She claimed he'd been through so much and had no recollection of me when she'd mentioned me to him. She didn't want him to be any more upset and hurt than he already was. The devastation all around was almost too much for us to bear. I was thankful that at least they had each other.

The only person I spoke to about Zane was Bianca. She had come with me to Weston a few years before as moral support. I wasn't supposed to see him.

I *especially* wasn't supposed to invite him back to my hotel room.

But the desire to have at least one shared memory with him was too much for me to resist.

He was the man I loved and for one night I got to bask in his forbidden arms. My father was the only other person who knew, and it wasn't information that he'd be looking to spread around. It frustrated him enough that I'd elected not to date over the years, despite his encouragement to move on. The only person who hadn't been pushing me to give up on Zane was Bianca. She understood, without explanation, that it wasn't an option for me.

She also understood that boarding that plane and going to see him was the one thing I'd been looking forward to for years and that even if he had moved on, I needed to see it with my own eyes.

Could I find it within my heart to be happy for him if he had?

I'd cross that if it came. And if I had no other choice, I'd smile, because that's love. You must find it within yourself to celebrate the other person's wins, even if they break your heart.

Chapter Three

ZANE

I walked past the bulletin board in the foyer of the Harmony Café. A poster for the local Halloween Gala caught my eye. I reached out and tore it from the wall and nodded over at Mark, my brother-in-law, who sat at our usual table with his coffee in hand, and he shook his head at me.

We met there most mornings before work ever since I got my own place a year before. I looked down at the poster in my hand. The Halloween party was only a couple of days away. Another Saturday night filled with disappointment?

No fucking thanks.

I'd had my fill of waiting all night for a woman that couldn't be bothered to show up for the past two years. For all I knew, she was married with kids. There I was, pushing forty, and I should have been doing the same. Instead, I'd made zero progress in the family building department. Why had I expected her to return at all? We'd spent one night together. It was a good night. But I had to accept it for what it was.

A hook-up.

If only I could convince my mind of that. The dreams were getting out of control. They felt all too real until they fell apart. And they always fell apart in the same way.

Up in smoke.

I crumpled the poster and tossed it in the garbage can on my way to the counter.

Heather stood behind it dusting her hands on her apron as I approached. All smiles, as always. "The usual?"

I scanned the menu board. Maybe I'd mix it up today. Who was I kidding? "Yup."

"One Americano coming up."

I paid, grabbed my drink, and sat down across from Mark. It was early in the morning, but Main Street was busy. There weren't any spaces available in the angle parking that lined the sides of the road.

When I'd first arrived in Weston four years before, I thought I'd just spend my recovery there. Living with Zara until I could return to Los Angeles. And while I no longer lived with her, I didn't see the point in returning to a city that hardly noticed I was gone. I'd had friends from the L.A. fire department contacting me in the early days, but as the years passed and I didn't return, they moved on. Besides, I didn't remember half of them. So I didn't bother going back. As far as I could tell, my life in Los Angeles had been a lonely one.

Mark set down his cup of coffee. "You had another dream, didn't you?"

I looked over at him. "Yeah, how'd you know?"

He scoffed. "Buddy, you always look like you've seen a ghost the next day."

"It's that obvious, huh?"

He nodded.

I let out a puff of air.

Fuck.

I *had* seen a ghost, at least, in a way. Because that's what she'd done, hadn't she? Ghosted me. She left with the promise to return and year after year she was a no-show.

Mark took a sip of coffee and a dribble ran down his beard. I wasn't too sure about him when my sister told me she was going to marry him straight out of high school. But he was a good guy. I was forever indebted to him, and thankful that he had taken me under his wing as an electrician, while I was unsure if I'd be able to return to being a fireman.

I'd joined the volunteer fire department in town, but we hadn't seen too much action. So far, I'd rescued two cats out of trees and put out a few fire pits that had gotten out of control. It was nothing like the action I'd seen in Los Angeles. If I was honest, I missed it. Even if it almost killed me. At least being an electrician paid well.

"Where are we headed today?" I asked Mark.

"The old motel by the highway. They had a rat infestation a while ago. They got rid of them, but it seems like they did some damage to the electrical."

"They should just condemn that dump."

He shrugged. "It's the only place to stay in town."

"Not true. There's the bed-and-breakfast."

"It only has four rooms."

"Yeah, I guess you're right."

I didn't want to set foot back in that damn motel. All it did was remind me of how much time I'd wasted hoping that the note my mystery woman had given me before she disappeared would come true. I'd asked around about her. She said she was visiting a friend in Weston. But no one knew anything about her. Then again, my description of the pretty blonde dressed as a sexy bumble bee was vague. She hadn't even given me her name. She held her cards close to her chest all night. I should have seen the disappearance coming.

Fuck, I was doing it again.

I ran my hand through my hair. That woman had consumed my thoughts for far too long. I glanced over at the coffee bar and Heather looked away.

She was cute, sweet, single, and, judging by the way she looked at me every time I was in there, interested. Mark leaned in. "I think she's hoping you'll ask her out one of these days."

"It ain't gonna happen."

I'd noticed her looking my way on multiple occasions. But I didn't want anyone's brand of cute, sweet, or sexy apart from the mystery woman's.

Zara said I should just wait until completing the rehabilitation treatment before I made any life-altering decisions. It was a heck of a tall ask. I was one session away from being done, and more than ready for my life to begin anew.

Now, if only I could've stopped myself from feeling like the woman that ghosted me had to be a part of that future. If only I could get the dreams to stop.

I was haunted by her memory most nights. But it was more than just reliving the night we'd spent at the local motel. In my dreams we were in love and happy. And I couldn't get enough of them. I woke up most mornings in mourning over losing her.

I thought about the Halloween party and sighed.

What's one more year?

I'd try again.

As long as I was in Weston. Or as long as I continued not to meet a woman that could hold a candle to my memories from that night. What other choice did I have?

I took a sip of my Americano. The black brew was almost as bitter as I was over the whole idea.

"Zane?" Heather's timid voice called out from behind me. I turned my head just as she slid a plate onto the table.

"I made them fresh this morning. The recipe is new. Try it and tell me what you think?"

I looked down at the sticky swirled cinnamon roll. "Thanks, looks good, but can you box it up for later?"

"They're best when they're hot out of the oven," Mark countered with a smirk.

Fucking shit starter.

I pushed the plate over to him. "Knock yourself out. I'll be in the truck." I grabbed my coffee and strode out of the café.

Heather was nice, but I didn't need anyone playing matchmaker. What they didn't seem to get is that if I wanted to make a move, I would have.

Chapter Four

PIPER

I set my bag on the bed and unzipped it before unpacking my things into the motel room drawers and taking a quick shower to wash the day's travel off me. My nerves were buzzing, or maybe it was the large iced coffee with an added espresso shot I'd had for breakfast.

It was only six days until my twenty-fifth birthday. The Halloween Gala I'd been waiting for, landed on the twenty-eighth this year—a few days too soon. But I'd made a promise, and I was determined to deliver as soon as I could. Besides, I couldn't wait another year.

I'd asked for the same room I'd stayed in three years before. It was sappy, but the dingy room with worn carpet and yellowing paint held memories of my happiest moments. And I needed comforting. I didn't know what I was up against.

What if he'd moved on?

He might have a girlfriend. Who wouldn't want to be with him? He was a catch.

My dad forbade me from staying in contact with Zara after the incident a few years prior. At which time he took over the financial commitment since he no longer trusted me to manage it. And I didn't want to risk Zane's treatment any more than I already had the last time I visited Weston.

There was a loud banging from the room next door, and the sound of power tools hummed through the walls. The motel had gone downhill since the last time I'd visited it and seemed in desperate need of repairs. Even the concierge, a sleazy-looking man with a comb-over, whose idea of customer service was to tell me to 'hold my horses' while he finished up an argument on the phone could use upgrading.

Either way, it would be the last time I would have to stay there. I didn't know how things were going to work out between Zane and me. He'd built a life for himself here and I had the one we'd once shared in Los Angeles still.

We'd have to cross that hurdle if it came. But I was getting too far ahead of myself. If the time was right, and we both wanted to make it work, we would.

The lights flickered, and the room plunged into darkness.

I felt my way through the pitch black to the window and opened the blackout curtains. I heard two voices emerge from the room next door. My skin goose-bumped the moment I set eyes on him, and I dropped down to peek over the windowsill.

Zane.

He was every bit as handsome as he always was. His dark hair had grayed a bit more over the years, but it only made him look more distinguished. Even though he was no longer fire fighting he'd kept his physique up.

He stood tall with his back turned to me, grumbling about something to the man I recognized as Mark, Zara's husband.

He turned, and I dropped the rest of the way to the floor, out of sight, when a knock sounded at the door to my room. My heart hammered in my chest. He was right outside. I couldn't see him yet.

It wasn't time.

Risking a few days was bad enough as it was. Almost an entire week? Forget about it. We were so close to being in the clear. They would send the last of the money to cover his medical bills in a couple of days and once I was twenty-five, my inheritance from my grandfather would unlock.

"Hey, is anyone in there? If you want power back, we need to get in."

No, no, no.

This couldn't be happening.

I heard Mark say, "I think it's empty. I'll go get the hotel manager to let us in."

Zane replied, "The shower was running earlier. Some-one's in there." They knocked again.

I ran to my bag and pulled out a tube of clay face mask, smearing it all over my face. Before I wrapped my hair up in a towel and tossed a robe over my clothing. "Coming! Just a minute."

My heart hammered in my chest as I unlocked the door, opening it. He couldn't recognize me so soon.

I made my voice higher than normal. "Sorry, I wasn't decent."

Zane tipped his head and scanned me down to my feet.

This was it. He'd discovered me, I was sure of it.

He furrowed his brow. I looked down to see what he had noticed. My jeans were peeking out from the bottom of the robe.

Mark stepped past me. "This may take a few minutes. The café around the corner is comping anyone a meal that's disturbed by our work here."

"Oh?" I said, turning my back to Zane, who hadn't stopped staring at me since the moment I opened the door.

Mark set a toolbox on the table. "Yeah, try one of the cinnamon buns. They're baked fresh."

Zane laughed. "You'll have to excuse my boss. He's what you might call a super fan of baked goods."

Mark patted his belly. "It's how I maintain my beach body. You're looking a little too ripped over there, Merrick. A good feeding might round you out enough for you to settle down with a good woman."

I sucked in a sharp breath and both the men looked over at me. I froze under their gaze. Zane was still single? I needed to maintain my composure as the overwhelming urge to squeal and dance in celebration overcame me. I allowed myself a polite smile. "Sorry, I thought I saw a spider." My heart was feeling lighter than it had in, well, years.

Zane walked past me. "If you go to the café, do me a favor and buy the place out?"

"Why?"

He laughed and crouched down to a panel on the wall. "Have you met the guy at the front desk?"

"Unfortunately, yes."

"Then you know why. He's footing the bill. In what I'm sure is the one friendly gesture he's made in his entire miserable life."

There was only one problem. I couldn't leave looking

like I did. And I couldn't risk taking off the mask and being recognized.

I moved to the bed, pulling back the covers. "I was about to take a nap."

"It's going to get loud in here," Zane challenged.

"I—I'm a sound sleeper." I slipped into the bed.

"Are you going to sleep with that stuff on?" He hovered his hand over his own face, referring to my clay mask.

Had he become a beauty expert in the past few years?

"It's a sleep mask," I said, turning over in the bed so my back was facing them.

One thing was for sure: I wouldn't get a wink of sleep. Not with him so close. But what else could I do?

He said nothing more, and they both got to work.

I had no other choice but to wait it out.

But I didn't mind. I took comfort in his quiet whispers and close proximity as they tried to keep it down for my benefit.

Chapter Five

ZANE

"Really, Zane? No costume again?" Zara pouted at me. I didn't enjoy disappointing my twin sister, but her love of Halloween and costumes was something we'd never seen eye-to-eye on.

"What do you mean no costume?" I pointed at my plaid shirt and jeans. "Isn't it obvious? I'm going as a lumberjack." I chuckled.

She rolled her eyes. "You are not. Besides, no one's going to get that unless you're carrying an ax. Oh, oh! That's it!" She jumped up from her seat at the dining room table and disappeared into the garage.

"They won't let me carry a weapon around all night, Zara," I called out while listening to her banging around in the garage.

"Oh, do shut up. I know it's around here somewhere. Just give me a minute," she yelled back.

A few minutes later, she came back with a plastic ax and a triumphant smile on her face. She set it down on the table in front of me. "I knew one of these days I'd get you to dress up. It's a pretty lame costume, but I'll take what I can get."

I picked up the plastic prop toy and flipped it over. "I'm not carrying this thing around all night."

"You sure as heck are. Come on, most of the time you can just leave it on the table."

I sighed. "Fine." It was a small ask, but the smile she gave me after I agreed made it worthwhile.

Would tonight be as disappointing as the past two years? I couldn't be sure, but I wasn't about to get my hopes up.

WE ARRIVED at the town hall early because my sister was on the committee and had roped both Mark and me into helping set up.

"Here," Zara said, handing me a box of decorations. Most of them she'd brought from home.

"What do you expect me to do with these?"

"Hang them around the hall." She shook her head like it was ridiculous that she even had to explain herself.

"I'd sooner hang myself. Isn't there anything I can do that doesn't involve decorating?"

She snatched the box back. "You'd screw it up anyhow. Go see if you can help set up the bar. They might need a hand carrying in the liquor."

Much better. Heavy lifting I could handle.

A couple of hours passed, and we were all done setting up. She'd convinced me to help with some decorations, but just the ones that involved a ladder. I had to maintain some level of dignity.

We crossed the street to have dinner at the diner before the party started.

I was eager to get back to the town hall.

Would this year be the year I'd get to see her again?

I was equal parts convinced of both opposing answers to that question.

I HEARD her before I saw her. The band was loud. But there was no mistaking that laugh. I'd dreamed about it so many times throughout the years. Searching through the crowd, I still couldn't find her.

Great, I'd lost my mind and was hearing things.

Had we reached the nightmare portion of the dream? I half expected the room to fill with smoke as echoes of her voice taunted me, only to wake up drenched in sweat and alone. There was a tap on my shoulder and I spun around.

It was Zara.

"Hey little brother, we need to talk."

We were only thirteen minutes apart but she liked to remind me that she was the older sibling.

"What is it?"

"There's something I should have told you." She took a deep breath and grimaced on exhale.

That's when I spotted *her*. Seated at the same table she'd been at three years before. I side-stepped my sister. "Sorry, this will have to wait."

"But, Zane, I—" She followed my line of sight. "Oh, I see it's too late."

I glanced at Zara out of the corner of my eye. We'd

need to have some kind of discussion later, but there was only one thing I wanted to do.

One thing I needed to do.

I crossed the room to her. Her red riding hood costume was the sexiest I'd ever seen. It even beat her little bumble bee costume from years before. Her tits were pushed high in a corset. A short red cape flowed over her shoulders, dusting the seat of her chair. She'd pulled her hair to one side, and it flowed out in waves from beneath the hood that sat atop her head.

Fuck, she was even more beautiful than I remembered.

And she was *real*.

She glanced around the room and I saw her breasts heave as she sucked in a sharp breath. My mind flashed back to the hotel room. The woman with the mud on her face. It couldn't be, but I was so sure by the shape her lips made that it had been her.

She stood from her chair to meet me. She was shoulder height on me even in heels. Too cute, as fucking curvy as ever, and she was back.

My ghost had returned.

She bit her lip. "Hey stranger, did you miss me?"

I grabbed her and pulled her to me. It wasn't a time for words. We'd get to those soon enough.

My ghost of a woman was corporeal again, and with her very real body pressed against mine I kissed her hello. My lips descended on hers without hesitation and she met my eager tongue with a quiet moan that reverberated through our kiss. Her lips were as soft and sweet as ever. I'd never been one for sweets but she was the one Halloween treat I craved.

I hope she knows that I'll never let her go again.

She pressed her hand against my chest, breaking our kiss. "Can we go somewhere more quiet to talk?"

"Of course." I took her hand in mine and led her out of the hall into the courtyard of the community garden next door. A local, Nico Andino, and his wife owned a landscaping business and had donated their time and resources to revamping it.

She smiled, looking around. Vines twisted around the two-seater swing. A fountain in the middle featured a cement fairy in mid-flight, dipping her finger into the pool below. Jack-o'-lanterns lit with candles decorated the steps that surrounded the base of the fountain. Locals had taken to calling it the wishing well and threw change into it to grant wishes.

Crazy, if you ask me.

"This place looks like it jumped right out of the pages of a storybook."

We sat down on the swing together and I looked over at her. "And so do you."

"I'd say the same, but it seems you've skipped a costume again this year."

I pointed at my chest. "Me? Never. I'm a lumberjack."

She laughed and my cock jumped with joy at the beautiful sound.

It felt like I was in another one of my dreams with her seated next to me.

But it was reality.

All the years left waiting, wondering, and biding my time were about to pay off.

I'd like to say I'd never lost hope. Or that with each dream that came and went up in smoke, I'd always believed we'd be right where we both belonged again, but there were times it felt so out of reach I couldn't help but lose faith in her return.

I reached over and pulled her hood away, revealing her

golden locks. I took a strand between my fingers and closed my eyes. Her hair was still as satiny and smooth as ever.

"Zane, I'm sorry it took me so long. But I need you to know that I had my reasons. You have to know that I never would have left you if it hadn't been necessary. I—"

I shushed away her explanations. "Let's not discuss it tonight. I just want to be with you. Tomorrow you can explain everything to me."

She smiled over at me and bit at her lip.

I reached out and cupped her cheek. "Because, this time, there *will* be a tomorrow. Am I making myself clear?" I paused, realizing I still didn't know her name.

She smiled at me. "Piper."

"Piper," I repeated her name. It was every bit as beautiful and delicate as she was.

"There will be a tomorrow this time, Piper. No excuses. No middle-of-the-night disappearances. Just us. From this day forward."

Her eyes lit up. "How can you be so sure?" There was hopefulness in them as she searched mine, but I wasn't sure why since I was making myself pretty clear. I also wanted to know why she'd gone to the lengths she had to conceal her identity from me the other day. But I'd set the rules. Tomorrow, whatever she had to tell me would come to light.

But tonight—tonight was ours.

Chapter Six

PIPER

We returned to the Halloween party together. The lights were dim, and a spotlight was on the stage where a master of ceremonies announced they were taking nominees for the costume contest.

He stretched his arm around my shoulders, pulling me close to him. "Once they announce the winner, we can leave, okay?"

"Zane, there's no way we're going to win."

"I don't know about that." He led us to a table and picked up a plastic ax. "You don't think that red riding hood and the huntsman have a chance?"

I bit back a smile and went up on tip-toes, wrapping my arms around his neck. "They have more than a chance." I kissed his cheek. "Just not at winning a costume contest." He poked me in the ribs and we laughed.

I missed how feminine I felt next to him. He was tall and broad, and just being near him made me appreciate my short and curvy body more. Or maybe it was because of the way he looked at me. It was hard to feel flawed in any way when I could see the admiration in his eyes. But the feeling was more than mutual.

Being in his arms again made me feel as though almost no time had passed at all. He was still the man I fell in love with years ago. And I felt hopeful that we could have a repeat of the past and that he'd fall in love with me all over again in time.

The only thing that made me feel a little nervous was that he didn't know the complete story. Would he understand why I did what I did? Why we'd kept the truth from him while he healed? How I'd made sure he had everything he needed?

Everything except for my love, but he couldn't remember that anyhow. It's hard to miss something you can't remember, isn't it? His lack of memory stung me, but I clung to the hope that he'd come through unscathed, and that his amnesia protected him from the intense longing that I lived with for years.

He'd always been a down-to-earth guy, and that's one of the many things I loved about him. He was a rare gem of a man to find in Los Angeles, of all places.

But it was also his blue-collar status that left my father with an unpleasant taste in his mouth about our entire relationship. A nasty taste that turned rotten when I told him about our fourteen-year age gap.

It was that combination that led to my father striking the deal with me he had. He'd promised anonymous donations of enough money to cover all of Zane's medical treatments as long as I agreed to step back from the relationship. With Zara on board, and Zane's amnesia standing in between me and him deciding together, what other choice did I have? It felt like the right thing to do.

I couldn't cover the expenses out of pocket and his insurance from the fire department didn't even come close to covering his injuries. The surgeries, doctor's visits, and rehabilitation. All of it was too expensive.

Zane lifted my chin. "Is everything all right?"

I nodded and swallowed hard, choking back the tears that threatened to escape me. I just hoped he could understand why I did what I did and not hold it against me.

He rubbed my back. "Would you like to dance?" The master of ceremonies had finished his speech and the live band returned from their break. It was the strangest mash-up of Halloween and country music I'd ever heard before. Not my taste by any means, but people seemed to enjoy it.

"I'd like that."

He led me out to the dance floor where we resumed our position, only adding swaying with the beat into the mix.

"We need to talk about you staying at the hotel."

He knew I was there? That could only mean one thing. He'd figured out my cover-up from the other day.

I smiled up at him as an unspoken shared moment of acknowledgment for what I'd done passed between us. "I'm booked there for another week."

"You won't be returning."

I wasn't about to argue with him, but I wondered why he'd brought it up. "I won't be?"

"No. First, if you think I'm letting you out of my sight for more than a trip to the washroom or something like that, you're mistaken. But it's also not safe for you to be there. The entire building has electrical issues. We'll grab your things after we leave here."

"Why are they still renting out rooms?"

"They shouldn't be. They brought us in to fix what we were told was damage from vermin. But I'm shocked the place hasn't burned to the ground already. All the wiring we've seen so far is faulty. The place needs to be condemned."

"That's scary. Is there somewhere else I could stay for the week?"

"There's a bed-and-breakfast, but you're mistaken if you think you're staying anywhere except with me. I'll give you the bed if you're not comfortable sharing it, but—"

I let out a sharp laugh. The idea of me doing anything except hopping into that bed and clinging to him, spider monkey style, was hilarious. Then again, he didn't know that. To him, I was just the woman he'd shared a one-night stand with.

He misunderstood my silence for contemplation. "If you're not comfortable with that, I can talk to my sister about you staying in her guest room."

"No, no, that won't be necessary. We'll pick up my stuff and go to your place."

He tipped his head. "You're sure?"

"I wouldn't have it any other way."

And it was true. We danced and after they announced Zara as the costume contest winner, we were free to leave.

After four years, I was going home.

Chapter Seven

ZANE

We came crashing through the door of my apartment. I felt around behind Piper for the light switch, our bodies still entangled as I flicked it on.

Her kisses coated my neck while I kicked off my boots and I hoisted her up. She wrapped her legs around my hips as I carried her to my bedroom and we fell back onto my bed. She was anything but demure. There was no hesitation in how freely she shared her affections with me.

It was the sexiest fucking thing I'd ever experienced. I propped myself up, looking down at her. Her eyes were an ocean of blue and me a willing sailor ready to get lost among them.

I'd been craving a second taste of this woman for too long. The desire to have my head buried between her thighs ripped through me. I wanted to claim her. To show her that even though she'd disappeared, there was never a moment that I hadn't wished for her to be mine and now that she had returned, she had little choice in the matter.

She arched her back. Her legs still locked around my hips as she ground against my hard cock. What was it about this woman?

She tore desires from me I hadn't felt about anyone in as long as I could remember. The urge to make her mine commanded me, and I sat back, reached up her skirt and pulled her panties away. She was still wearing her heels. "These can stay," I said, lifting her leg up and kissing her ankle just above where the strap encircled it. She sucked in a sharp breath.

I unbuttoned my shirt to pull it off. She grabbed the hem. "Leave it on."

I smiled. "Does Little Red want to get railed by the huntsman?"

She smirked and gave me a nod.

I flipped her skirt up, revealing her pink-shaven pussy, and licked my lips. "What if I'd rather be the big bad wolf that's come to eat you?" I ran my fingers between her folds, finding her clit. She arched her back, moaned, and rocked her hips in time with my hand. "Would you like that, babe? Because I want a taste."

She gasped as I worked her clit, swiveling her hips, pressing her pussy harder against my hand. "Yes, oh yes, please, Alexander."

My full first name?

No one, apart from my mother, had ever called me that. And she only ever did it when she was mad at me. People had decided it was cuter for my sister and me to have almost matching names while we were still babies. But my legal name remained unchanged.

How did she even know it? I'd only ever introduced myself to her as Zane.

But it was her tone that shook me to my core because it reminded me of a dream I'd had only weeks before where she'd called me that. Had we met before the Halloween party a few years ago? Fuck, I was insane for even thinking about it. I'd never contemplated fate, or destiny before, but if there was anyone that would make me believe in it—it was her.

Tomorrow, she would answer my questions.

I stroked her hair, her gaze unfocused.

I nibbled a trail down her inner thigh until my mouth was between her legs. Her moans punctuated my every move. I spread the lips of her pussy with my hand, exposing her clit, and flicked at it with my tongue. Her body shuddered as she cried out. She was so fucking wet I couldn't wait to dig in.

She tilted her hips to meet my mouth, and I rewarded her by circling her clit and lapping at her until she tensed up and, after only a couple of minutes, broke against my tongue.

Someone was eager.

The sweet cries of her ecstasy filled the room. Hopefully, my neighbors were sound sleepers.

My cock was rock hard in my jeans, begging for a turn at her. But maybe our talk couldn't wait after all. I couldn't stop thinking about how she called me Alexander.

Had I met her before?

Was there some truth behind the dreams? Were genuine memories mixed in and I didn't know it?

Chapter Eight

PIPER

Zane paced the floor at the foot of the bed.

He didn't interrupt as I told him the entire story. About the accident. How Zara didn't want to upset him further by letting him know that he'd forgotten me, his fiancée, thanks to retroactive amnesia from the head trauma he'd received when the beam fell and left him concussed and unconscious in a burning house. How my father hadn't approved of our relationship but promised to pay for his treatment. And how I was waiting until he was done with treatment or I turned twenty-five and had access to the inheritance that my grandfather left to me—whichever came first. How in a cruel twist of fate we had to wait the full four years until we could attempt to be together again.

"I think I remember you."

"You think? What do you mean by that?"

"I've been having dreams ever since we had that night together. There were dream aspects mixed in, but I can't help but feel like there was some truth tucked away in them."

"Like what?"

"Your favorite food is fettuccini Alfredo with basil."

I smiled. "That's half true."

He frowned. "I was so sure that I'd be spot on about that one."

"Oh, you're right. I love Alfredo with basil, but it's only my favorite when *you* make it."

He turned and left the room.

He seemed to take things in stride, but what if he was just putting on a brave face? The longer he was gone, the more I worried he was more upset than he let on.

When he returned, I looked up at him and asked, "Is everything okay?"

"It's more than okay, wouldn't you agree?"

I chewed at my lip. "We have so much that we need to go over and so many things that we need to sort out before we can even contemplate picking up where we left off. You need to get to know me from the ground up, for one. And second—"

He put his fingers to my lips. "Stop. I fell in love with you once, Piper, I'll do it again. When I asked you to marry me, where were we? How did I do it?"

"We were at home."

"Where in the house?"

"In the bathroom." I laughed but quit when I noticed his frown. "What's wrong?"

He paced some more. "In my dream, I was going to ask you in the kitchen."

I gasped and patted the bed next to me. "Sit down

Zane, it's dizzying watching you pace back and forth. Let me tell you the story."

He sat down next to me and placed his hand on my thigh.

"We were supposed to go on a weekend getaway. I didn't know at the time that you'd planned to propose. They had slammed me with a new project on Friday that I needed to get a head start on over the weekend, so when I came home, I asked you if we could reschedule our trip to the mountains. You were so accommodating. I never would have suspected that I'd destroyed your plans at all. You told me you'd make me dinner instead. That we'd have a cozy romantic evening and then you'd leave me be to get my work done over the weekend."

"What was I making you?"

"My favorite."

"Just like in my dream."

"I couldn't wait until after dinner to get my hands on you. It had been such a long day, and I wanted to unwind."

"And I made you wait."

I grinned. "No, you hoisted me up on the counter and we made love right there in the kitchen. But I guess we were a little too into it because the rolls you had in the oven started burning and when you spun around to retrieve them, you ended up knocking the pan of sauce all over yourself. You went to get cleaned up in the bathroom and I followed. Just before you pulled your pants off, you took the ring box out of your pocket. Then you apologized to me and said you couldn't wait any longer and that you'd be proposing to me in your boxers. You said life could get messy sometimes, but that the one thing that would always remain constant was us. And that was it. You asked, and I said yes."

I didn't want to tell him that two days later he'd been called into work and tragedy struck for us.

"The old me did the right thing. I'd do the same today."

"*If* you didn't need some time to heal over this…"

"I've had years to heal, Piper. That's all I've been doing. The last thing I want to do is feel wounded about something else in life. Especially when I have the choice not to be. You did what you thought was best. Sometimes we have to make tough choices in life and it's hard to tell what's right or wrong at the moment. Other times, it's not even clear in hindsight. But none of that matters. What matters is that you're here now. You kept your promise and returned."

"So, you aren't upset that I did what I did?"

He kneeled in front of me and placed both of his hands on my thighs. "I wouldn't say that I'm not upset. There are a lot of things upsetting about the fact that they kept us apart. I'm not impressed with your father. And I'm going to have a word with Zara about boundaries."

"I think she meant well. It was a tough time. She was only doing what she thought was best for you."

He gave my knee a squeeze. "I get that, but the decision should have been ours to make, Piper, and it wasn't. But I'm going to fix it."

He gave me a wide grin and reached into his pocket, pulling out a ring. My heart hammered in my chest. It was his grandmother's. I recognized it because it was the same one I'd worn once before. Zara had asked for it back, and as much as I would have liked to keep wearing it, it only seemed right to return it.

I shook my head. "Wait. When did you get that?"

"When I left the room, I grabbed it from my fire safe."

My heart raced, looking down at the diamond solitaire.

It was a classic style. As everlasting as our love. But the bundle of nerves forming in my stomach cautioned me against getting my hopes up. Zane didn't remember me; he couldn't be ready for a commitment, could he?

He held the ring out toward me. "Marry me?"

Chapter Nine

Piper cuddled up close to me as I stroked her long blonde hair. She'd asked for a breather after my proposal. I wished being close to her was enough to make me remember. But I couldn't dwell on that. Not when the present was more than enough. We could replace every memory I had lost with a new one.

Because I finally had her.

The girl of my dreams.

And I would never let her go again.

I smiled down at her as she watched the movie. I couldn't hold it in any longer. There was no point. Here goes nothing. "Have you considered my proposal?"

She shot up and sat back, looking over at me. "Zane, it's too soon. You don't know me."

"Is that a no?"

"Well, no, but…"

"Yes, it's fast, you're right. But if the accident hadn't happened, we'd be married by now, don't you think?"

She nodded. "Yes, I can almost guarantee that."

I reached out and took her hand in mine. "You've haunted my dreams for years, baby. I'm ready to make actual memories with you. A lifetime of them."

Her lips twitched. I could tell she wanted to smile. I could tell she wanted to say yes as badly as I wanted her to, but she'd been through so much since the accident. She'd lost just as much, if not more than I had, because she had to live life knowing what she had lost.

I was fucking tired of losing. Nothing could come between us again, and I had to make sure of it. Not her family. Not another traumatic event. And especially not fear.

She squeezed my hand. "We can have forever without rushing through the steps our old selves would have taken. I'm not going anywhere. Never again. I promise you."

"The bottom line is, I'm still me and you're still you, and we're meant to be. My mind may have forgotten you, but my soul never did. You occupy it. No amount of head trauma could erase you. We've suffered because of it and I just want us to have all the things that we should have. We deserve it. Say yes, and I promise you that for as long as we live, you'll never regret it."

A tear ran down her cheek and I swiped it away with my thumb before gathering her in my arms.

She sucked in a long breath. "You're sure about this, aren't you?"

"I've never been more sure about anything in my entire life."

A bright smile overtook her face, and I knew at that moment I had her.

"Yes, Zane, I'll marry you."

"Oh thank goodness, babe. Because, for you, I'm not too proud to beg."

She laughed. "Maybe I should have held out a little longer just to see that. The great Zane Merrick on his knees begging for my hand."

I narrowed my eyes at her as I slipped the ring on her finger. It fit her like it was made for her. "Keep it up, baby girl, and you'll be the one on your knees."

She bit her lower lip. "That's not a bad idea."

I sat forward and pressed pause on the remote. This woman was half vixen and half angel, but all mine. "Pumpkin, stick with me and you'll soon find out I'm full of good ideas."

She slid off the couch and pressed her perfect body between my knees. "I always loved your ideas." She placed her hands on the front of my jeans, petting at the visible outline of my shaft.

It twitched with need, craving her hot mouth.

Fuck me.

I'd missed her touch so much. She unzipped my pants, pulled my hard cock from them, and paused, hovering just over the tip. She looked up at me with a sly grin on her lips.

What a tease.

I reached down and grabbed a handful of her hair. "Don't you think I've waited long enough?"

She stuck out her tongue and swirled it around the head and I groaned, shutting my eyes, anticipating more of her hot, wet mouth, my balls tight and aching with need.

Nothing.

I peeked at her.

There was that naughty little grin again. It made me want to just force her head down and make her choke on it. Fuck, I needed to feel her again. "What's wrong?"

"Why would you think something is wrong?" Her eyes danced as she gave the tip another flick.

She was just as much of a tease in reality as she was in my dreams. I hadn't imagined that part after all. "Again, don't you think you've made me wait long enough?"

She looked up like she was thinking about it, then let out a little laugh before grabbing my shaft and damn near swallowing it whole. My hand tightened in her hair as she bobbed and sucked.

Fuck.

It had been so long since I'd been with anyone. She was my last and knowing we were engaged before my accident, she'd likely been the only woman I'd slept with in quite some time.

She swirled her tongue around the tip and gave it a hard suck.

I groaned. "You love sucking my cock, don't you, babe?"

She made an 'mmm' noise but refused to stop to reply. She looked so hot wearing her little Halloween costume. The way it pressed her tits up to where they were almost overflowing over the top of the corset made me want to tit-fuck her until I came all over her naughty curves. Just thinking about it combined with the way she was fucking me so hard with her mouth had me ready to burst.

"If you keep that up, I'm going to cum."

I half expected her to relent. To tease me some more, but I was thankful when she didn't, and deep-throated me instead.

That was it.

I couldn't take a second more and I filled her luscious mouth with my hot seed.

She pulled back, opened her mouth, showed me the creamy white liquid that she'd just milked from me before swallowing it back, and smiled. She was filthy, but sweet, and the combination was driving me wild.

If I hadn't already asked her to marry me, I sure-as-fuck would have after that display.

I couldn't wait to discover all the other reasons I'd made her mine once before.

Chapter Ten

PIPER

"What are you doing?" I asked Zane as he grabbed my bag and placed it by the door. "We're leaving."

It was still Halloween night, and we hadn't slept yet. "Now? Where are we going?"

He leaned against the door frame to his bedroom. "You'll find out in the morning."

"Why don't we just leave in the morning instead?"

He shook his head. "No can do, Princess." He turned and continued into his room and I followed him to watch as he grabbed a duffle bag and started filling it.

He wasn't the impulsive type before, but this new Zane fascinated me. Instead of trying to argue with him, I sat at the foot of the bed watching him pack.

"I don't sleep well in cars," I said.

"Good, then you can keep me company."

"How many hours is this trip?"

"Around six."

"Are we headed north? South?"

"Keep asking questions and I'll blindfold you for the drive."

"Yes, Sir." I mock-zipped my lips and twisted the key.

He nodded and turned his back to me to continue packing. "That's my good girl."

Good girl? He really didn't remember much about me, did he?

I looked down at the red riding hood costume and pulled the bow that held the corset closed loose and pulled it away from me. Leaving me naked from the waist up. I didn't feel like showing up wherever we were going doing the walk of shame. "Can I at least change first?"

He glanced at me over his shoulder and froze with a bundle of socks in his hand. That caught his attention.

He tucked them in the side pocket, zipped his duffle bag, tossed it on the floor beside the bed, and stalked toward me.

"I was going to wait until…"

He was so close I could feel his breath on my face. The heat in his stare threatened to turn me into a puddle of desire where I stood. "Until what?"

"Nevermind." He wrapped his arm around my waist, pulling me close. "It seems like my girl has other plans in mind."

My heart swelled at him calling me his girl. I'd waited years to hear him say something like that to me again and it felt like a sinful dream coming from his lips. For too long, his love, touch, and gaze were forbidden.

The relief I felt being in his arms again overwhelmed me. That he was so determined to make me his while making up for lost time was more than I ever could have expected. It was almost as though the years apart had never happened. We were only missing one thing. "Zane?"

"Yes, Piper?"

"Make love to me?"

His gaze softened. It was like I'd hit a switch in him. He pressed a lush kiss against my mouth, tugging at my bottom lip. I leaned into the kiss and he lifted me up and set me back on the bed, removing what remained of my costume. He stripped bare, revealing his chiseled chest and rock-hard erection. The wetness between my thighs grew.

It had been so long since we'd united as one. He leaned over me, hiking up my leg and positioned himself at my opening. He ran his hand over my breasts and I moaned. "You're gorgeous, my love." He grazed my nipple with his lips until it pebbled and he took it into his mouth, sucking and running his tongue over it. "I've been dreaming of being inside you again."

I ran my hand through his hair, admiring the added gray that time had deposited on his head. It only made him look more handsome. "Me too."

"Did you wait for me, baby?"

"Of course, I did." And it was true. I couldn't imagine being with another man apart from Zane. I'd given him my whole heart years ago and there was no undoing that, no matter what life tossed our way.

He pressed into me. "So, this pussy is all mine?"

"All yours."

He groaned and pushed deeper, stretching me. I circled my hips, trying to feed more of him into me. He smiled down at me, realizing what I was trying to do, but he didn't hold back. It wasn't a time for teasing. We'd both waited so long to be intimate again. He pressed the rest of the way into me. "You're so tight."

I clamped down on him and he rewarded me by

finding my clit and massaging it. His fingers were adept as he worked in and out of me, never breaking eye contact.

In his eyes I saw the love I had for him reflected back at me. Was it too soon? Maybe. But it was also irrefutable proof that our love transcended time and circumstance. That despite him not remembering, he spoke the truth, his soul hadn't forgotten me—or us.

We continued making love, locked in our embrace until I felt the warmth of pending release wash over me, climbing to the surface. I pulled him closer, hugging his neck as he buried his face into my hair.

My body shuddered. I didn't want it to end so soon because it had been so long, but he felt too good. Another shudder hit as I attempted to hold my orgasm at bay for as long as possible.

"Let go, baby girl. Let me feel you come around me."

I did as I was told and let all of that energy burst out of me with abandon. He sped up thrusting in and out of me until he came right along with me.

He laid down beside me and I shuffled over, turning until he was spooning me with his arm wrapped around my chest.

I felt so safe and happy in his arms I could have laid there forever. But we had a trip to go on.

Somehow, I knew without asking that forever was part of the travel itinerary.

Chapter Eleven

ZANE

We arrived in Las Vegas and went straight to get a marriage license. Was I moving too fast? No. She was mine, and I wanted to make it official as soon as possible. I wouldn't let my woman get away again. "Zara and Mark are flying in tonight to witness tomorrow. Is there anyone you'd like to invite?"

"I spoke to my best friend, Bianca, but she's in France right now and I can't think of anyone else."

"We can always host a reception at a later date for anyone you wanted to come that couldn't. My world is pretty small, so I don't need it, but if you do, we'll do it.

She shook her head and gave me a quick kiss. "No. It'll be perfect, just the four of us." She gasped. "I—I don't have a dress."

"It's Vegas. There must be bridal boutiques. We have a whole day to figure it out."

"That's not enough time for tailoring."

"You could show up in a garbage bag and I'd still be the luckiest man alive. Or you know, you could just wear your red riding hood costume again."

She slapped my chest. "I am not getting married in a cheap Halloween costume."

I grabbed her hand and pulled her close. "You'll find something. Whatever makes you comfortable. It doesn't matter. Do you want me to come with you?"

"Isn't that bad luck?"

"I think we've maxed out on bad luck, don't you?"

"You never know."

He sighed. "I'm not a fan of you roaming around Las Vegas by yourself. How about you wait until Zara gets here and you two can go together?"

"You want me to wait until tomorrow to buy a dress?"

"I do. Is that going to make you panic?"

"A little, yes."

"Okay, new plan. You choose the shops and I'll escort you around but you can shop alone. Does that work for you?"

Judging by the grin on her face, I was sure it did.

WE'D ALREADY BEEN to two stores with no luck and decided it was time to take a break and grab lunch. Besides, I had some good news for her I couldn't wait to share.

"I hope you have room for me in your home."

"Always. Why?"

"Because I'm coming back to Los Angeles with you on Monday."

"But what about Mark and your work with him in Weston?"

"He understands. I'm thankful for everything that he's done, but it's time I get back to the life I shared with you."

She took a bite of her sandwich and chewed. "What do you mean by 'get back to'? You aren't saying that you're—"

"Returning to the Fire Department. That's what I'm saying. I spoke with my supervisor there. Told him I'd been keeping fit and volunteering with the fire department in Weston. He said he'd be happy to have me back as a part of the team."

She set down her sandwich and pushed away her plate. "You should have discussed this with me first."

"Why? It's my career. I always planned to go back to it if I could."

She pouted and looked around the restaurant, blinking a few times in rapid succession. Was she about to cry? "I see. Well, I'm happy for you."

But she looked anything but happy.

"I can't spend my life being afraid, Piper. I need to get back to helping people. Those guys saved my life when they pulled me out of that house. And thanks to your sacrifices I've healed up better than the doctors anticipated. I can't help but think I need to go back. I think you know me well enough to know that I'm not the kind to walk away. That includes my work with the fire department."

"It almost killed you."

"Every day when you leave your house, there are risks. Every time you hit the interstate or board a plane, you're taking your life into your own hands. And it doesn't stop there. Even when you're at home there are still risks. Life is a risk, no matter how cautious you try to be. Did I think I'd get injured the way I did? No. But I knew that every time I walked into a burning building to rescue people who couldn't rescue themselves that I was taking that risk. But was my willingness to take it needed? Of course, it was. My reward was in the face of every family I reunited. Even though they were losing everything they had, I could see their relief. They still had each other, Piper, and that spurred me on. That's why I chose the work I did. I'm sure you know I lost my parents in a house fire."

"I do," she said, her chin quivering.

"Then you know how important it is to me that I continue saving lives."

She fanned her face and let out a long exhale. "Yes, I know. Can we talk about something else right now, please? I don't want to cry in public."

"Of course, babe." I moved my chair around the table to sit closer to her and took her in my arms. "You just need to trust in me."

"I do. And always have, Zane. It's just a lot to process right now. If you were to stay in Weston, would you still be happy volunteering and working as an electrician?"

"I would, but that's irrelevant. Your life isn't there, and neither is ours."

She nuzzled her face into my chest. "True. Unless—"

I shushed her and rubbed circles on her back. "Don't. It'll be okay. I can't promise you I'll never get hurt on the job again. But I also can't promise you that nothing bad will happen for the rest of our lives. But what happened has held up our lives for long enough. It's time to move on."

She frowned. "You're right. It *is* time to move on."

I kissed the top of her head. "I'm glad you understand, babe. Finish up. There is a dress to find."

We went to the last store, and I popped into the grocer next door that sold wine and a few other things. After shopping we needed to move on to the celebrations.

Tomorrow was the first day of the rest of our lives.

I waited an hour for Piper to finish up in the shop. She

hadn't taken that long in any of the other stores. I waited another twenty minutes, hoping it meant she'd found a dress, before I set foot in the store. I glanced around and she was nowhere to be seen. The shopkeeper, an elderly woman with reading glasses perched on the tip of her nose, was behind the counter with a novel.

"Where's the woman that was in here?"

"The curvy blonde?"

"That's the one."

"Oh dear, she left a long time ago, she only spent a few minutes in here, before I told her we don't carry her size. She mumbled something about it being a sign and left."

I spun on my heels and dashed out of the store, scanning the street. But in my gut, I knew she was gone. I returned to the hotel. There was a note on the bed with the ring set on top of it and her things were gone from the suite.

Zane,

I'm sorry. I was wrong to think that things could work between us after so many years. Too much time has passed.

Please take care,

Piper

I grit my teeth, crumpled the note, threw it in the trash, and shoved the ring in my pocket.

Fuck me.

No, she was not disappearing again.

I wouldn't allow it.

The last time she left, she didn't leave me anything to

go on. But this time was different, and she hadn't held back. I knew her name. I knew where she worked.

And I knew enough to know that she was the woman I'd spend the rest of my life with.

This time, I wouldn't let her get away with it.

Chapter Twelve

PIPER

I thought about taking the week off of work. The mountains of paperwork that had piled up over the few days that I was gone agreed that it was the right choice for me to return early. It was that or drown my sorrows in romantic comedy movies and copious amounts of takeout food.

No, I needed to move on, because moving on meant that Zane wouldn't rejoin the Los Angeles Fire Department. It was safer for him to continue living the life he had in Weston than to return to the city and pick up where we left off.

I loved him way too much to allow that to happen.

My dad poked his head into my office, knocking on the door frame. "You busy?"

I sat back in my chair. "Always, but come on in."

He stepped into the office and took the seat across from

my desk. "Where'd you run off to? Our pilot said he took you to Arizona and picked you up in Nevada. Las Vegas, of all places. Is there something you need to tell me?"

"No, nothing. I just needed to get out of town for a bit."

"To Tucson? Which is close to where your ex-fiancé lives. I'm going to give you another chance to tell me the truth, Piper Ann."

I didn't want to tell him the truth. It was his fault I had to hide anything from him. But it had become second nature.

"Yes, I went to see Zane."

He narrowed his eyes at me. "And?"

"And nothing. Too much time has passed for things to be rekindled. He has a whole new life there. It's the outcome you were hoping for. Happy?" I lowered my gaze to my desk.

He sighed. "I understand you're upset, but I don't appreciate the hostility."

"She's taking it too easy on you if you ask me."

My head snapped up and there Zane was leaning in the doorframe to my office, with his arms folded across his chest.

He came for me.

That's not what I had planned for, but a part of me was relieved to see him there.

My father stood. "How'd you get in here?"

Zane glanced at him and scoffed. "You say that like it's hard. You're overdue for your fire inspection."

I pressed my lips together and bit down on them, trying not to laugh.

My dad straightened his suit jacket and puffed out his chest. "I'll be having a word with the Fire Chief after this stunt."

Zane shrugged. "Can't say I didn't expect this response. I know how much you enjoy destroying lives. Or—" He placed his hand on his chin in mock contemplation. "—Is it *controlling* them?"

"You're overstepping, son."

Zane put his hand up, signaling that my father had said enough. "I'm here to see your daughter. We already know you're unreasonable. I'm not looking to waste either of our time. There's the door." He pointed behind him.

My father pointed at my phone. "Piper, call security."

"Leave, Dad," I said.

My dad's jaw dropped as he turned to look at me. "Excuse me, young lady?"

"He'll be leaving soon. But you need to let me talk to Zane alone."

He stepped toward Zane. "Not until I get a thank you. You know who paid for all your medical bills, don't you?"

Zane nodded. "I sure do. And you're right, I need to say thank you." He looked over at me. "Thank you, Piper."

My dad let out a haughty laugh. "Is that what she told you?"

"No, she told me what you did, Sir. But she paid for it with her freedom. She made decisions she wouldn't have if not for you forcing her hand. There's more value in the sacrifice of human happiness than there is in money. But we both know that's a lost concept on you. If it weren't, you would never have forced her to do what you did. You wouldn't have kept us apart." He locked eyes with me. "We need each other. We're meant to be together. And that's not something time or distance can change. You've sacrificed a lot, Piper. And I know why you did what you did. I was asking you to give up your peace of mind and that wasn't right. You made your hesitations known, and I forced the issue. I realize how wrong of me it was to do that. That's why I asked to be moved over to inspections. Guess which unit was hiring, babe?"

"Which one?"

"The film unit." He looked over at my dad. "Do you know what that means, *pops*?"

My father grimaced because he knew as well as I did what that meant. It meant that Zane was a part of the unit that was going to issue permits for our on-location shoots or special effects.

My dad guffawed. "This is blackmail."

"You would know all about that, wouldn't you?" Zane smirked at him. "It's fate if you ask me. Besides, I'm not asking you for anything except for the opportunity to make your daughter happy with or without your blessing. What do you say?"

My dad threw up his hands. "It seems I was only avoiding the inevitable."

"Dad?" I asked. He had to have more to say about it than just that.

"Piper, I thought I was doing what was right for you. But it's clear you two will wage war to be together. I'm unimpressed. "

Zane smiled over at me and I returned it before addressing my father. "Well, I'm impressed. But I suggest you leave right now, Dad, because I'm about to make up with my fiancé and you won't want to witness it."

He grunted and left my office, slamming the door behind him.

Zane tipped his head. "Was that his way of giving us his blessing?"

I laughed. "Close enough."

Zane approached me. "So, I'm guessing you're happy with my solution, then?"

I pushed my chair back and stood. "Thrilled. I'm sorry I ran from you, Zane. I just couldn't stand the idea of—"

"Piper, please, don't. I didn't listen to your concerns. I was thinking only about what I wanted. How I wanted more than anything for us to pick up where we left off, but I went about it wrong. I wasn't thinking about how my choices might impact you. You've been through enough and I need you to know, babe, that no matter what, I'll always do whatever it takes to make you happy. But you need to promise me something before I put this ring back on your finger."

"Anything."

"If I'm ever being thick-headed like that again, you need to let me know. I'm going to make sure I involve you in decision-making from now on, but if I ever fail to, I need you to remember you have every right to put me in check."

"I promise."

He rounded my desk and went on one knee. "Third time's the charm, right? Piper, will you marry me?"

"Of course, I will." I collapsed onto his lap, straddling him, and threw my arms around his neck. He rolled back on the floor with me in his arms and we laughed together.

"This isn't how I expected this proposal to go."

"Nothing ever goes how you expect it," I said. "But it's perfect."

His smile faded. "I love you, Piper."

"I love you too, Zane. I've loved you since the moment I met you."

"How did that go?"

"We have a lifetime ahead of us. I'll fill in the blanks in time." I rested my head on his chest and he wrapped his arms around me, hugging me close.

The path of our love wasn't how I'd ever imagined it

would be when I met him at a mutual friend's wedding all those years ago. But it was finally our turn.

And if there was one thing I was sure of, it was that we'd always make it through together, no matter what challenges life threw our way.

Epilogue

ZANE

ONE YEAR LATER

"Congratulations, brother." Mark patted my back, his other arm around Zara. I looked over at Piper.

"Thank you." She looked gorgeous in her wedding gown. Our relationship and wedding had been perfect.

As much as I wished the memories of our previous relationship would return to me, they never did and the dreams had stopped. I had to accept that the fragments of the past that I had were all I would ever have. But it didn't matter when I had her in the present.

We waited a bit and planned a wedding. As much as she said she was okay with eloping, I felt like she wanted a proper wedding, and judging by her relaxed expression as a couple of her bridesmaids fawned over her and her dress across the room—I was right.

Her friends from work, mine from the department, and our family were all in attendance. Her father included. I scanned the room for him. He was sitting there with his wife. Once he realized that Piper and I were in it for the long haul, he came around. Did that mean that I forgave him for everything he had done to keep us apart? It wasn't important. We were together, and that was all that mattered.

Once I knew she was mine, there was no way I was going to let her go again. She'd received her grandfather's inheritance soon after our engagement, but she continued working at the studio. Her parents were aging and all of that would be hers sooner rather than later.

But my wife was ambitious. She'd taken her money and started a foundation for victims of amnesia and their families to provide financial support and access to other services to ease the transition. We had more than enough, so we asked that instead of gifts, guests donate to the cause.

Zara hugged me. "She's the perfect woman for you, Zane. I'm so proud to call her my sister-in-law."

I smiled down at my sister. Any minimal upset over what had happened had long since settled between us. Piper was right. She only did what she thought would make things easier on all of us. With any luck, the foundation would provide people with the support to make facing those kinds of decisions a lot easier.

I locked eyes with Piper. Myles Reeve, an actor from her studio, approached her. I grit my teeth since she'd told me he had eyes for her. "You'll have to excuse me. I have to go see my bride now," I said.

I crossed the room to her and put my arm around her

shoulders. Why did she even invite him to our wedding in the first place?

"Do you think I've got a chance with her?"

Myles glanced over at a bridesmaid. I guess I misread the situation. Thank goodness, I didn't want to be dragging the guy out of my wedding reception by the ear—or worse.

Piper laughed. "I don't see why not." She leaned into me and dropped her voice. "Can we get out of here yet?"

I gave her a kiss. "Of course, my love."

We made our way to the stage, announced our departure and informed guests they were welcome to stay longer to enjoy the bar. Then we snuck out the back where her car was waiting to take us to the airport. We were flying overnight to Bora Bora to stay in an overwater bungalow her best friend Bianca, a hotel heiress, had arranged for us to stay at.

PIPER

I LEANED back in the lounge chair on the sundeck and put on my sunglasses to shield my eyes while I looked out at the stunning turquoise waters. The skirt of my white linen dress fluttered in the breeze. There'd be a lot of work waiting for me when I returned to Los Angeles, but being on our honeymoon made it more than worth it. He returned from within the bungalow with a glass of champagne for each of us. Bianca's father was a celebrity chef, so the food at the resort was five-star. I took a sip and the bubbles danced in my mouth, matching my already light and effervescent mood. Being there with him after everything, made me want to pinch myself just to make sure I wasn't dreaming.

But it wasn't a dream.

It was us. We had everything we'd hoped for and more. I established the foundation. He had a new, safer job with the fire department, but he was still saving lives by preventing incidents. We had my father's blessing. There wasn't a single thing that wasn't going our way, and after all the struggles we had faced, I felt blessed to say that.

He leaned over my shoulder and moved the skinny strap of my dress aside to kiss along my collarbone, and a jolt of desire ran through me. I couldn't believe how lucky I was to be with the man of my dreams on the vacation of a lifetime.

He nuzzled his face into my neck and let out a low groan. "Would you like me to run us a bath?"

I leaned my head on his. "Do you even have to ask?"

"I expect you inside and naked in ten."

"Yes, sir."

"Bring that good girl attitude with you."

I laughed. "Don't tempt me to change it."

He stood. "Maybe I'll be the one to do the teasing for a change."

I pulled my sunglasses down, peering at him over the top of them. "Doubtful. You haven't been able to resist giving me everything I ask for, yet."

He grabbed my arms and lifted me from the chair to meet him in one fluid motion. "Is that so?"

"It is."

"Maybe it's time I do a little less giving and a lot more taking." He grabbed my ass and backed me to the table on the sundeck before spinning me to bend me over it. He gathered my skirt, pulling it up, baring my naked behind.

"Zane, right out here? What if someone sees us?"

He pulled his cock from his lounge pants and slapped my ass with it a few times before slamming it into my wet pussy.

"Fuck, babe. It's like a slip-and-slide. What's got you extra turned on? Don't tell me my perfect girl likes the threat of being seen."

I moaned as he thrust in and out of me. "And what if I do?"

He slapped my ass, and I yelped. "Then you're not the good girl I thought you were. Trying to flaunt your pussy for the entire world to see, are you?" He slapped my ass again and slammed into me hard and fast. "I can't have that, now can I? What if they think it's not mine?" I couldn't imagine anyone thinking I wasn't his with him buried as deep inside me as he was. "What would you tell them?"

"That—" He grabbed my tit and leaned into me to get deeper and I cried out.

"What would *you* tell them?" He groaned. "Fuck, babe, tell me what I want to hear."

"I'm yours," I screamed. "I'd tell them I'm all yours."

"Fuck yes, that's what I wanted to hear. And I'm about to spill every drop of cum I have in you because your pussy is mine too, isn't it?"

"Yes. All of me."

He went hard and fast until he wrapped his arm around my hips and leaned over, hugging my back filling me as promised.

When his breathing slowed, he pulled back and let my dress fall back down, covering me. He stumbled back and collapsed onto the lounger with a satisfied sigh. "Come here."

I took a few steps, and he pulled me the rest of the way onto his lap and gathered me into his arms. "We'll take a bath soon. I just need to rest for a few minutes." His eyes fluttered closed and a couple of minutes later he drifted into a post-orgasm coma. I didn't care. It was Zane. I knew he'd make-up for it later. He always did.

I let my eyes close and I soaked up the rays. The sun's warmth blanketed us as we lay in each other's arms.

We had a lifetime ahead of us. Some day our family would grow, and we weren't taking any precautions to prevent that, but at that moment things were perfect with it being just the two of us. Enjoying each other's company in whatever way we pleased, whenever and however we wanted to.

I nuzzled my face into his chest and he tightened his grip on me further. He held me a little closer ever since I'd ghosted him and I held him a little closer to make up for the memories he'd lost. Even though we both knew forever was the only option for us.

Also by Lia Preston

RELATED BOOKS

Where Liberty Dwells: Heart of a Wounded Hero

RETURN TO WESTON AND JOIN LIBERTY, ON HER STEAMY SECOND-CHANCE ROMANCE JOURNEY WITH HER BROTHER'S BEST FRIEND, NICO.

Chasing Glory: A Curvy Girl Age Gap Instalove Prison Romance

RETURN TO WESTON AND JOIN CHASE ON HIS TABOO ROMANTIC SUSPENSE JOURNEY WITH HIS DOCTOR, GLORIA MOORE.

MAN ON A _MISSION_ SERIES

Miss Conduct: A Curvy Girl Age Gap Instalove Romance (Man on a Mission: Book 1)

JOIN PAIGE AND HER SILVER FOX BOSS, RHYS, ON THEIR SPICY FORBIDDEN ROMANTIC JOURNEY.

Miss Education: A Curvy Girl Age Gap Instalove Romance

(Man on a Mission: Book 2)

JOIN ELLE AND HER SEXY IRISH PROFESSOR, FINN, ON THEIR KINKY FORBIDDEN ROMANTIC JOURNEY.

Miss Fortune: A Curvy Girl Age Gap Instalove Romance

(Man on a Mission: Book 3)

JOIN BRIDGET AND HER BEST FRIEND'S BROTHER, HUNTER, ON THEIR SPICY SECOND-CHANCE FORBIDDEN ROMANCE JOURNEY.

Where Liberty Dwells

HEART OF A WOUNDED HERO

CHAPTER ONE

Liberty

"You're dating *him* again?"

As Nico shook his head, a lock of dark hair fell into his eyes. Though, his expression remained neutral I sensed a storm brewing behind it.

Maybe.

He stuffed his hands in his pockets and looked away as we walked in downtown Tucson, past an inner city park that might have been nice if not for the dried-up fountain, sun-crisped greenery, and worn-out gazebo.

Nico had two ways of being, tough to read and impossible to read.

I bit my lip, not knowing how to respond, or if I was even meant to. Or maybe I was trying to avoid the conversation I dreaded having with him most.

There was a lot to consider, and I knew Nico wouldn't understand, but I wanted to try. "I think Paul has changed.

He hasn't dated since we broke up and he says he misses me and he's sorry."

Nico scoffed. "I don't trust him and neither does Chase. He cheated on you, Libby."

Shame washed over me, but I couldn't keep myself from glancing over at him. He was twenty-nine, young looking and towered over me. It was no wonder he joined the Army and was about to start training for the Ranger's. His body was both lean and strong, built for agility and combat. What *was* a mystery was how he was both pretty and manly looking at the same time. It's alarming how easy on the eyes he was.

Alarming because I'd known *of* Nico my entire life, though from a distance. He'd been my older brother's best friend for decades. I'd not seen much of him until recent years because his father moved them around depending on where he was stationed. But the bond Nico and Chase shared never wavered. They maintained their friendship mostly through online games, and it strengthened even more when Nico moved back to Tucson four years ago. When they tired of working dead-end jobs and enlisted together at twenty-five-years old.

I should have felt out of place as a 20-year-old woman hanging out with her much older brother and his group of Army friends, but I didn't. And out of everyone, Nico and I'd become inseparable, a fact that hadn't escaped Chase, who'd issued us a very stern warning a month prior to *not* get involved. Then again, Chase didn't approve of any guy who wanted to date me.

Still, I didn't let that stop me from hanging out with Nico, and considering we didn't live in the best neighbor-hood, Chase didn't mind that he escorted me places. But as much as I loved spending time with Nico, I needed to spend *more* time with guys I *could* date. I looked skyward and hoped the clouds looming over us weren't a bad omen brought on by my recent decision to give my ex-boyfriend a second chance.

A crack of thunder roared overhead, followed by an instant rain shower.

Okay, that had to be a bad omen.

Nico grabbed my elbow and pulled me through the nearest park gateway.

"Run," he said, pointing toward the dilapidated gazebo to our right.

We both jogged to evade the fat droplets. I stumbled up the steps, and he reached out for me, pulling me to him. My chest heaved against his, but I was alone in my labored breaths from our dash for shelter. He was far more fit than I was. I looked down at my white cropped t-shirt to see it had turned translucent from the rain, revealing the crimson lace bra I wore beneath. He followed my eye line and sucked in a breath before taking a half-step back.

I laughed and brushed the now wet lock of hair out of his eyes. "One of us should start carrying an umbrella."

He smirked. "As if it'll matter now. I'll be gone soon and you'll be seeing someone."

Frowning, I pulled at my shirt, hoping to hide my bra —it didn't help. "It won't be like that. I know you're my brother's best friend, but you're important to me. I'll always make time for you."

"Yeah, if you say so, Lib." He paused. "I'm sorry. It's not that I don't believe you. It's just that I don't believe it for a fucking second that the prick has changed. I want to see you happy with someone. But my gut is telling me it won't be with him. Besides, when Chase finds out, he's going to rough him up. You know that. He still hasn't forgiven him, and never will." He huffed. "Neither will I."

So far, our conversation was going about as well as I suspected it would.

I sat down cross-legged on the wooden slatted floor of the gazebo. He pulled off his leather jacket and sat down next to me, hanging it over my shoulders as we looked out toward the fountain in the middle of the clearing. I traced the surrounding path with my eyes before leaning my head on his arm.

He had to be wrong.

Paul wouldn't dare put me through that all over again, would he? But what if he did?

I was already nervous about Nico's upcoming training and deployment. He'd become my rock in a very short amount of time. He was different from the other guys in the group. There was a seriousness about him that made him stand out. If I ever needed anyone to talk to about anything, he was my go to. Could I really face another failed relationship attempt without him? If it didn't work out with Paul it would be Nico that I would want to console me. It was his guidance I would want above anyone else's. His shoulder I'd want to lean my head on when uncertainty weighed heavily on my mind. It made my skin prickle to think it, but I had to let go of that feeling. It wasn't fair to either of us.

Yes, dating Paul might turn out to be a bad idea. But unlike Nico, I wasn't a six-foot stoic god of a man that could have had any woman *if* he wanted her. I was just a five-foot-five girl with a cute face (so I'd been told), and more curves than most guys seemed to know what to do with. Or maybe I was kidding myself and they were more curves than most guys wanted.

Either way.

I needed love, and sure Paul wasn't perfect, but it was better than the alternative of sitting around and waiting for some Prince Charming to come whisk me off my feet. No, waiting wasn't an option. I wanted to date. To fall in love and experience the entire whirlwind of emotions that came along with it. Even if getting back together with Paul was foolish, I needed to take the chance rather than live life wondering what *may* have been.

Nico turned his head, kissing the top of mine. A rare gesture from him. The last time it happened was when my mother passed the year before and both he and Chase came home for a couple of weeks of rest and relaxation. Losing Mom was tough. I think that's why Chase took me under his wing like he did. He just wanted to make sure that without her around, I'd be okay. And I was, thanks to Chase and, later, Nico.

The head kiss confused me, though, because I didn't need comforting, or I shouldn't have. I was starting a new relationship. It should have been an exciting time. So why did I feel like the dark clouds weren't only looming in the sky that night, but between Nico and I? Was he—no, he couldn't be—why did it feel like he was kissing me goodbye?

A lump formed in my throat as I looked up at him. He dropped his eyes, looking back at me. His lip twitched into the faintest smile, revealing an almost never seen but highly sought after dimple. He only had the one, but then again he only ever half-smiled, at most, so maybe there was another one hidden behind that stubble that I'd never seen. There was something so bittersweet about the moment that my chest ached in abstract longing.

He sighed. "I want you to know I'll always be around…"

"Why do I sense there's a 'but' coming?"

He groaned and dropped his arm from my shoulders.

"Because you know me. Even better than I know myself sometimes."

I shook my head. "You don't have to do this, you know."

"Neither do you. But you're doing it. And I won't watch. No, I *can't* watch. If you're going to go back to Paul, you'll be facing it alone. I can't watch the woman I—" He paused. "—my best friend's little sister self-destruct."

"Don't. Just don't. Why are you doing this? I'll be okay. I'm older now. Stronger. Wiser. I can handle myself. Just, please, don't pull away from me."

"Do you want to know why?"

"I do." My phone buzzed, and I reached into my purse, pulling it out. The caller id flashed Paul's name. I set it on my thigh, still ringing. I'd call him back in a minute.

Nico grabbed my chin, tipped my head up to him, and placed a firm kiss on my lips.

What the…

My chest thudded with panic, stealing my breath away. I looked down at the still buzzing phone with Paul's name taunting me on it. Guilt washed over me.

Nico hopped up. "That's why."

"Nico, I—"

He cut me off and pointed at the phone. "And you may as well take that. Because we both know that's what you want to do."

My jaw went slack. I didn't know what I wanted to do. On the one hand, I'd waited a couple of years for Paul to say the things he'd told me earlier that day. It felt like vindication. But I'd never imagined Nico and I would become as close as we had. Or that he would feel any kind of way about me, let alone want to kiss me.

The phone kept buzzing. I looked down at it and back up at Nico. Speechless. Why did he wait until now to do this? Did he want me, or was he just trying to keep me from seeing Paul again?

He ripped the phone from my lap with a growl and pressed answer. "For fuck's sake, man, we'll be there in a few," he said and hung up the phone before tossing it into my lap. I'd never heard him bark out at anyone like that before. He crossed his arms over his chest, biceps popping out. "Well?"

"Well, what? What do you expect me to say now?"

"Anything. Something. Tell me to fuck off or that you never want to see me again. Tell me you can't date him now. Or, shit, tell me you feel the same way. Fucking anything, Lib! Anything to put me out of my misery."

"What misery? This is the first I'm learning of this. You never seem miserable around me." The rain started easing up, fewer and fewer droplets disturbing the surface of the small puddle that had developed in a dip in the pavement just outside the gazebo.

"That's because I'm around *you*. Why not choose me? Tell me why?"

"I don't know. I didn't think this was on the table for us. What about Paul? Or Chase? He'll lose his mind if he hears about this. Have you thought about that?"

He nodded. "That's a lot of excuses you have at the ready. You're right then. It isn't on the table for us. Forget I did that." He reached out his hand to me. "Come on, let's get out of here before the rain starts up again. I'll walk you, but I'm skipping the party. I've embarrassed myself enough for one night." He pulled me to my feet.

"You haven't. Please come."

"Can't."

"Why not?"

"Because Paul's going to be there and if I see him lay one fucking hand on you, or even smile in your general direction, I'll knock his teeth out. Is that something you want?"

"Well, no, but…"

"Then you go alone. Do what you've gotta do."

I wanted to just throw caution to the wind. To tell Nico that I thought we had a chance. That Chase *might* accept us. But I didn't believe it. He was bad enough about me dating guys my age. There was no telling how he'd react if I dated his best friend who was pushing thirty.

Even knowing all of that, a part of me wanted to stay right there and sort it out with Nico. Maybe we could work it out? But Paul was waiting for me. We were already forty-five minutes late. It all felt so overwhelming. And even if by some miracle I could choose Nico, I at least needed to go end it with Paul. If that was even what I wanted to do. Nico and I both needed a bit of time to reflect before taking things any further. At least, I knew I did. "Okay, let's go, then." We stepped out of the gazebo, walking through the park, before starting back down the road. The rain reduced to a drizzle.

I glanced over at him and he returned my gaze through thick dark lashes and for the first time, my heart swelled in a new way for him. A way that I couldn't accept without consequence.

Had I known he'd stop taking my calls and move away, I would have skipped the party, and that's what I should have done.

But I *didn't*.

And that was the last time I thought I'd ever see Nico Andino.

CHAPTER TWO

Nico

FIVE YEARS LATER

I parked my truck out front of the white a-frame in the historic district. The neighborhood was the last piece of Weston's suburbs left untouched by developers and their oversized modern homes. The area would have been a developer's dream if not for soft ground that ran the length of the backyards, rendering half of each property unstable. I'd had more than a couple of build permits declined in the neighborhood.

My assistant, Cody, hopped out of the truck ahead of me. He was always eager to impress and way more of a morning person than I was. I took a few more sips of coffee before meeting him at the tailgate. "You grab the gear. I'll go have a chat with the homeowner."

Abby, my office manager, said the job order was for an addition on the house. A sunroom, to be exact. But there was a problem. I was looking right at one. She must have got her wires crossed. Maybe we were removing it?

Fuck, I hoped not.

It would have been a shame to do anything to the house that ruined its original character.

I walked up the path toward the well-maintained home. The glass was new and the structure sound. It was looking like they might be another pain-in-the-ass homeowner with ridiculous expectations. But, it was nothing new. It was the life I'd built for myself after my injury forced me out of the military. And, I was damn proud of what I'd built. Still, the house was just about as nice as it could be for its age. Any changes would've messed with perfection at that point.

I knocked before noticing the doorbell and pressed it for good measure.

A muffled woman's voice called out from inside. "Coming."

I turned, looking past the manicured lawn and down the street at the row of old houses. The sun was high in the Arizona sky. It was another blistering hot one.

Then again, when wasn't it?

The door creaked open behind me. "Hi, sorry to keep you waiting."

I turned to face her and took one step forward before stopping. Wide, blue eyes and a cascade of brown hair framed her heart-shaped face, a smear of clear gloss topped her full, kissable lips. Lips that adorned a face too familiar to forget. "Liberty?"

What was she doing here? When had she moved to Weston from Tucson? I leaned back and checked the house number. 765. I had the correct address. There was no doubting that.

"Nico!" She stepped forward out of her house wearing a white terry cloth robe tied tight around her waist, accentuating her generous hourglass shape, and gave me a tight hug.

I stood still.

As still as a stone statue.

Unable to return the gesture out of sheer shell-shock. "It must be my lucky day. Yours was the first construction company I called. And I didn't even know it. Small world, isn't it?" She rattled on, weaving a strand of chestnut hair through her fingertips.

"It sure is. When did you move here?" Something about the situation made me think it was anything but a coincidence, but I played along.

She stepped back into the house and motioned for me to come in. "Three weeks ago. I'm still getting settled, so don't mind the mess." I crossed the threshold into her living area. What mess? There were only a few boxes stacked along one wall.

I ran my hand through my hair. "Abby said you needed a sunroom? But—" I pointed over my shoulder.

She chewed at her bottom lip. "It's small."

"It fits the house."

"True, but I pictured more space for greenery."

I laughed. This was coming from the woman that couldn't keep a silk plant alive back in the day.

A wide smile broke out on her face. "I know what you must be thinking."

"So you've learned how to keep plants alive, have you?"

"Yes and no. I've just found the right plants for me. Succulents. Low maintenance, but I need the sun to do the heavy lifting."

I furrowed my brow. "How many succulents does one woman need?"

"Enough for my fairy gardens?"

Well, now I'd heard it all. "What in the world is that?"

"My business. Come, let me show you." She led me through the house and out the sliding glass door that led into the backyard. There was a table with several ceramic planters filled with scenes. Houses made of logs, tiny glass toadstools, little wooden swing sets and blue stone ponds. All miniatures with clusters of succulents arranged among them.

"Wow," I said. Although, it didn't surprise me one bit that she'd chosen to do something like that. Minus the plants, that is. "Geez, when I left, you were studying to be an accountant."

She scrunched up her nose. And she might as well have just hurled a dagger at my heart because I'd let myself forget how freaking cute she looked when she did that.

"It wasn't for me."

"I could have told you that." And, I had. But the thing about Liberty was that she loved exploration. It was just hard to tell her that maybe every fleeting interest didn't *need* to become a career. Or that she could take an interest in something without having to throw herself headlong into it.

She blinked. "So yeah, I need some more plant space. It's cheaper to grow my own than it is to buy everything from a nursery. Can you help me?"

I looked out at the spacious backyard. "How about this? We leave the house as is because you'll be kicking yourself if I put some big eyesore of a sunroom on it. And instead we build you a greenhouse? It'll be cheaper too. Not as many materials needed and if we keep it modest, there's no need for a permit."

She threw her hands up. "Now why hadn't I thought about that?"

Because she rarely thought things through? Or at least that used to be true. But I'd loved that about her. How unpredictable she could be.

Until it hadn't worked in my favor.

I shrugged. "I'll get my assistant in here. We'll take some measurements and I'll draw up some schematics tonight for your approval in the morning."

"Sounds perfect. Coffee tomorrow then?"

I paused. Caught up in the subtle pout of her lips as she waited for my reply. I swallowed hard.

Her eyes went wide. "To go over the schematics, of course."

"Uh yeah, sure, coffee'd be great." My eyes dropped to her hands. No wedding ring. I heard that she'd married that idiot Paul and divorced him a few years later. A five-year-old anger simmered in me like a pot coming to a boil. He'd fucked up again, hadn't he?

"Nico? Are you okay?"

She knew as well as I did that I wasn't.

At least, not *yet*.

None of this was okay. Her moving to my town. Me showing up on her doorstep. It was the furthest thing from 'okay'. I'd thought about how it would feel to see her, but not knowing her intentions made things harder. All it did was make me register my loss all over again, and wish that things could have been different and that we could get back the years we'd wasted.

Or, better yet, that I'd gone to that party with her and knocked his teeth out like I said I would. Because then maybe it would have prevented whatever heartbreak brought her here…

To me.

That was the bottom line, wasn't it? She could try to pass this off as a coincidence as much as she liked, but she was in Weston because it was over with him and it wasn't with *me* yet. The question was, for what purpose? I'd told her, that last night, that I'd always be there for her. That I was only out of her life as long as she was with him. And even then I hadn't planned on keeping my word because I hadn't planned on staying away from her period. But when I'd gone to Chase and told him what had happened and how I felt about Liberty, all I got was a black eye and told to 'stay the fuck away from my little sister'. I could have fought back, and won, had I not respected the guy so much. That my love for her pushed me to cross the line at all with him spoke volumes. There was no way I'd be okay with standing on the sidelines again as I watched her carry on with the next idiot.

The only thing that was for sure was that I'd have a few days of construction time to figure it out.

"Seriously, Nico, are you okay?"

"I'm better than I've been in years, Lib." And standing across from her it was true. As much confusion as I might have felt, I couldn't ignore the fact that it was my chance. My chance to get what I'd always wanted. To prove to Liberty just how well I could love her. Whether Chase approved was irrelevant to me. We hadn't talked since I made it into the Rangers and he didn't and blew up at me.

Cody came around the side of the house. "There you are."

I introduced them before informing him of the change of plans. "Get your measuring tape out."

Liberty smiled. "I'll go get you two something cold to drink. It's too warm out."

I put up my hand, stopping her. "Save it for tomorrow. We won't be long today."

Her smile faltered. "Oh, that's right."

"But we'll be back tomorrow." Or at least I would. I wasn't about to pass up the opportunity to get one-on-one time with her. Besides, I only needed Cody around once the construction began. My back couldn't handle all the crouching or kneeling anymore.

She tried to contain her smile and gave me a nod. I didn't know what tomorrow would bring, but I felt I wasn't alone in hoping it would be something good.

I hope you enjoyed this sample. You can find the rest of Nico & Liberty's story, Where Liberty Dwells, at:
books2read.com/wherelibertydwells

About the Author

Lia Preston is a new author of short contemporary instalove romance. She loves writing body-positive stories about curvy heroines in forbidden romance scenarios with their sizzling hot alpha heroes.

She was diagnosed with ADHD as an adult and aims to provide readers with quality romance stories that cater to shorter attention spans, busy lifestyles, or those who need a palate cleanser between longer reads.

She has much more in store for her readers and can't wait to share it all over the coming years. If you're a fan of paranormal romance, Lia has a fantasy fanatic alter ego, Luna Preston, who'll be releasing her debut next year.

Visit www.literarylovepotions.com for more information or join her on any of the social platforms below.

amazon.com/author/liapreston

facebook.com/literarylovepotions

instagram.com/literary_love_potions

bookbub.com/authors/lia-preston

tiktok.com/@literary_love_potions